The ENCHANTED BRIDGE

ALSO BY ZETTA ELLIOTT

Dragons in a Bag

The Dragon Thief

The Witch's Apprentice

DRAGONS in a BAG
— BOOK 4 —

The ENCHANTED BRIDGE

ZETTA ELLIOTT

ILLUSTRATIONS BY CHERISE HARRIS

Random House　New York

Visit us on the Web! rhcbooks.com

Educators and librarians, for a variety of teaching tools,
visit us at RHTeachersLibrarians.com

Library of Congress Cataloging-in-Publication Data
Names: Elliott, Zetta, author. | Harris, Cherise, illustrator.
Title: The Enchanted Bridge / Zetta Elliott, Cherise Harris.
Description: First edition. | New York: Random House, [2023] | Series: Dragons in a bag;
Book 4 | Summary: "Jaxon and his friends are back in the magical realm, Palmara, trying to convince Guardian Sis that magical creatures should exist in both worlds, but things might be even more complicated than Jax and his friends realize"—Provided by publisher.
Identifiers: LCCN 2022004679 (print) | LCCN 2022004680 (ebook) |
ISBN 978-0-593-42774-3 (trade) | ISBN 978-0-593-42775-0 (lib. bdg.) |
ISBN 978-0-593-42776-7 (ebook)
Subjects: CYAC: Magic—Fiction. | Dragons—Fiction. | Witches—Fiction. |
Apprentices—Fiction. | African Americans—Fiction. | LCGFT: Novels.
Classification: LCC PZ7.E45819 En 2023 (print) | LCC PZ7.E45819 (ebook) |
DDC [Fic]—dc23

The text of this book is set in 12.75-point Chaparral Pro.
Interior design by Megan Shortt

Printed in the United States of America
1st Printing
First Edition

For
those who live
between worlds,
linking one
to another

1

___

With fire, there is light.
With fire, there is heat.
The fire within us is ancient.
It has burned for thousands of years.
Our flames can unmake what
    was formed from hate.
Our ashes allow life to triumph over death.
Those who covet our power will try
    to seize it for themselves.
Our power must be protected,
    for our power will save this world.

2

Everything happens all at once. I am falling. I am flailing. I am mired in a pool of tar. I am soaring among the stars.

When time is linear, one thing happens after another. When it's not, things get messy!

I brought us here. I wanted to be a leader and my friends followed me to Cloud Gate in downtown Chicago. I have been given an important mission by the Supreme Council. I used to have another job, but now I am the ambassador who will convince the Guardian of Palmara to open the portals linking her realm to ours. I am going to free the magical creatures being held against their will. I failed as a witch's apprentice, but I won't fail again. Will I?

These thoughts swirl in my mind like a tempest—who I was, who I am, who I will become. I hear the fear and panic in my friends' voices as the mirrored surface of the bean-shaped sculpture presses us to the ground. We are being flattened against the pavement. We are being sucked into a sticky blackness that stifles our screams. We are floating weightless in a distant galaxy. It can't be happening all at once and yet . . . it is!

I feel frightened. I feel angry. I feel guilty. I led my friends straight into this trap, and I can't do anything to help them.

My stomach sinks with the weight of my shame. Then it lurches as the giant silver bean starts to spin! The treacherous wizard Ol-Korrok cackles as we clamor for help.

"Ah, dear guests, you have finally arrived! I have waited for this day for a thousand years. Let me say it again: you . . . are . . . welcome!"

Suddenly, there is silence. The spinning sensation stops. I try to breathe, but it feels like my mouth—my entire body—is smothered by feathers. I think my eyes are open, but all I can see is a blackness so complete that it's impossible to tell which way is up. I can't see or hear my friends anymore, but I sense that they are close by. I reach for them, but my fingers only feel the softness of feathers. Then I hear the gentle voice I have heard so many times before in my dreams.

"Be patient, my son. We're nearly there."

He is not my father, and I am not his son. *Beware the crow*. I should have listened to that warning when I had the chance.

I take a deep breath and reach out once more, hoping to grab hold of something. To my surprise and relief, I think I see stars sparkling overhead. The nauseating sensation of everything happening all at once recedes. The blanket of feathers thins, and I think I feel solid ground under my body. Before long I'm able to stand.

I am here. This is now.

With my sight restored, I realize that I am alone. I call out the names of my friends. "Vik? Kenny? Kavi?"

The silence frightens me more than the darkness. I remember the phoenix and reach inside the pocket of my hoodie to make sure that it's okay. It opens its eyes and looks around, clearly curious. Then it lifts itself into the black sky and starts to grow! The tiny bird that could fit in the palm of my hand spreads its wings and burns so bright I have to shield my eyes with my arm. It's like a small sun radiating intense light and heat. Then a gust of wind sends the phoenix tumbling through space.

I look over my shoulder and see Ol-Korrok grinning as the golden bird—my last ally—disappears in the distance. He is dressed in a simple black robe tied loosely at his waist with a white sash. The stars above ring his bald head like a crown, but as he gazes down at me, Ol-Korrok almost seems . . . humble. Nothing like the flamboyant figure I met in Chicago or the jeering wizard who trapped us inside the bean.

Seeing the suspicion in my eyes, the wizard holds up a finger, and I wait just a couple of seconds as he transforms into the small black-and-white bird from the trial. The crow perches on my shoulder and says, "Perhaps

you prefer this form. You like birds, don't you, Jaxon?"
Before I can answer, the wizard shifts again and stands
beside me in his monkish black robe. Where the crow's
talons dug into my shoulder, I now feel the pressure of
Ol-Korrok's long fingers.

"What have you done with my friends?" I demand
angrily.

"They are unharmed," Ol-Korrok assures me. "I
merely sent them ahead with a gentle nudge—as I just

did with your remarkable phoenix. We'll catch up with them eventually."

I peer into the darkness and realize we are standing on a narrow clear surface. I would call it a bridge except that it doesn't seem to link anything. The first time I traveled to the realm of magic, Ma was with me and I couldn't see anything from inside the guardhouse that served as our transporter. When things went wrong and we wound up traveling back in time instead, Ma was there to use her witch powers to make things right. The next time I stepped inside a transporter, my grandfather was there to make sure we reached the magical realm. Now Ma's back in Chicago and Trub is missing. Until I find my friends, I'll have to deal with this wizard by myself.

"Palmara didn't look like this before," I say warily, missing the massive baobab trees I saw on my first visit.

Ol-Korrok nods. "That's because we aren't there yet. First, we have to cross this remarkable bridge that I built with nothing but grit, dedication, and, of course, a little enchantment." The proud wizard pauses, and I realize this is my cue to compliment him on his achievement but I refuse to flatter him. Ol-Korrok clears his throat and continues. "I do apologize for the bumpy ride—this is a prototype, really. It still needs a few tweaks here and there."

Somehow his embarrassment helps me to relax a little, and I let Ol-Korrok guide me along the invisible bridge. It feels like we're strolling through the Milky Way. I'm still upset about being separated from my friends, but my curiosity is getting the better of me. "Are we in outer space?" I ask.

The wizard raises his arm and sweeps his hand across the glittering expanse of stars. "This . . . is Source."

"Source?"

He lowers his arm and smiles patiently. "Everything comes from something. You and I, your friends, your realm and mine . . . all of it came from this. I wanted you to experience it for yourself so you would know just what it is we're fighting for. Magic mustn't be reduced to card tricks and silly potions. This majesty is the root of all things magical, Jax. This is the root of life."

It's pretty hard to hide the awe I feel as I walk along the enchanted bridge with Ol-Korrok. The terror I felt when entering Cloud Gate starts to feel like a distant memory. There are many questions I'd like to ask the wily wizard, but I remind myself that I am not on vacation. I have to think about the others, too. I embarked on this journey with my friends, and they're still no-where to be seen.

I start to walk faster, but Ol-Korrok tightens his grip on my shoulder, forcing me to match his leisurely pace. "There's no rush."

"I need to find my friends," I insist. "They're probably worried about me."

"I doubt they've even noticed you're missing," Ol-Korrok replies. "By the time we reach them, only a few seconds will have passed since you last saw your traveling companions." I give him a doubtful look, but the wizard just winks and adds, "Time is rather elastic here."

I watch as Ol-Korrok plucks a star from the sky. When he releases it, the star shoots across the blackness as if launched from a slingshot. I squint to see if I can spot my friends up ahead, but there seems to be no end to the darkness.

"They're there," Ol-Korrok assures me, "even if you can't see them. You and your friends share a unique bond. You can feel that they're close, can't you?"

He's right—I can. The wizard speaks softly and without all the dramatic gestures that marked his performance before the Supreme Council. "Why did you send them ahead?" I ask with a little less hostility.

"So I could speak privately with you, of course! Your friends would have asked endless questions, which I'm happy to answer. But I suspect they'd rather receive their guidance from you. Some people just have the innate qualities of a leader, and that's why others are drawn to them. Your friends depend on you, Jax—you know that." When the wizard realizes he can't charm me, he tries a different approach. "I suppose, if I'm honest, I'd have to admit that I didn't want to have to share you with them! I've waited for this moment for a very long time."

"You talked to me in my dreams."

"I did," he admits. "I just wanted to introduce myself, really. But now that we're finally together, we can get to know each other better."

I hate to admit it, but I *am* curious about Sis's mysterious twin. "Blue already told me what happened to you," I tell him. "Why did you change your name?"

The wizard sighs. "It's a strange feeling when your reputation precedes you. Especially when you have a reputation like mine."

"Seems like you're famous—in Palmara, at least."

"*In*famous—that's not quite the same thing," he says. "But I haven't answered your question: Why did I change my name? When my sister banished me to the Forgotten Tower, she stripped me of most of my powers. You have no doubt seen her shape-shift."

I nod, remembering how frightening Sis was when she arrived in Brooklyn as a huge dragon. The wizard smiles ruefully and says, "I, too, could transform myself into the fiercest dragon. But I found when I traveled among the people that a less intimidating form allowed me to observe without instilling fear in others. My favorite form was the pied crow. My cousins here in North America are black all over, but I chose a bird with white feathers. The Maasai in East Africa call such crows ol-korrok, after the sound the birds make. Soon they began to call me that as well, and the name stuck."

Mama always told me it was disrespectful to call someone out of their name. I wonder if the once-powerful wizard minded having his name taken away from him.

Ol-Korrok responds as if he just read my mind: "In a way, I was grateful to have a name other than Ranadahy, which bound me to my sister and her cruel sentence for my supposed crime. Have you ever felt like people made up their minds about you before they even met you?"

"Sure," I say without hesitation. "For a long time, people felt sorry for me. I wasn't Jaxon the geography whiz. I was that boy who lost his father in a stupid car crash. And sometimes when Mama and I go shopping, the security guard watches us like we must be up to no good just because we're Black."

Ol-Korrok shakes his head. "It's so unfair! I knew you'd understand. You know, Jax, it's been a long time since I've had a friend. The Forgotten Tower is probably the loneliest place on earth. My only company was the birds that occasionally came to my window, but I couldn't unburden my heart to them. The loneliness sat in my chest like a boulder, aching endlessly."

I already know that Ol-Korrok is a talented performer, but right now he seems sincere. I'm actually starting to feel sorry for him. "Did Sis ever visit you?"

"Not once in a thousand years," he replies dejectedly. "Nor did anyone else. The Forgotten Tower is aptly named. It no longer appears on maps of Palmara, and none remain who might remember the treacherous route to its locked door."

"So . . . how did you escape?" I ask.

The wizard shrugs. "I was not as friendless as I imagined myself to be. When word reached me that my sister was losing support, I decided I must act. Not out of a desire for vengeance but in order to save the creatures I have only ever sought to protect."

"If that's true . . . then why did Sis banish you?"

Ol-Korrok clasps his hands behind his back and sighs heavily. "Exile has changed me, Jax, and shown me the error of my ways. I see now that my sister was right to punish me for jeopardizing the creatures in our care. I don't blame her, really—not anymore."

I must look surprised, because he laughs and says, "I've had a thousand years to forgive my sister. Was I angry when she first imprisoned me? Of course. And I remained bitter for a long time. But I could not deny the charges made against me."

The wizard points at the dark sky overhead, and suddenly the stars start to arrange themselves in shifting scenes just like an Etch A Sketch! I listen to Ol-Korrok but keep my eyes up above as the glittering diamonds bring his story to life.

"I accepted an offer from a deceitful king in your world who craved power more than peace. When his fine promises turned out to be false, I felt ashamed that I had let my trusting nature blind me. I apologized for forging such an unwise alliance and even fought alongside my sister to dethrone the scoundrel. But Ranabavy would not be appeased. I could have challenged her—demanded a trial by combat. But I knew I could never

14

hurt my beloved twin. So I accepted my sentence and bid farewell to all I knew and loved."

I want to ask a hundred questions, but it would be rude to interrupt the wizard, so I swallow my curiosity for now.

"In time, I came to understand how fear operates," he tells me. "It's a powerful force, Jax. Fear has shaped our world in astonishing ways."

I think about all the wars fought just because one group of people feared another. "Fear makes people irrational—and mean," I say.

"Precisely!" Ol-Korrok exclaims. "Unlike my sister, I have always tried to see the good in people. Ranabavy treats every new person she meets like a potential enemy. Perhaps that's what is required of a guardian. But the burden of keeping Palmara safe has taken its toll on her. Sadly, you were never blessed with a sister, but I know how much you love your mother. Your father, too." When I glance up at him to gauge his sincerity, Ol-Korrok smiles at me and adds, "You don't stop loving someone just because you can't see them anymore."

I know exactly what he means. Sometimes I feel like I love my dad even more now that he's gone.

Ol-Korrok gazes up at the sparkling stars and says,

"You probably know that twins share a special connection. My sister and I have been together since before we were born. Nothing can truly separate us. Much as she may wish to be rid of me, I will never abandon her, for I know she cannot rule alone—the burden is too great for one person to bear."

"I don't think Sis sees it that way," I say as tactfully as I can. "What if she doesn't want a family reunion? What will you do then?"

"I will find another way to serve Palmara and prove to my sister that I am a changed man. Before sending me into exile, she allowed me to take one book from our extensive library of magical texts."

"Just one?"

The wizard nods. "I knew every word by heart after the first year. But it took over five hundred years for me to truly understand the message behind the author's wise words."

For a while, we walk in silence. I wait for Ol-Korrok to share the lesson he learned from his book, but it seems that's one thing he wants to keep to himself. "I like to read, too," I tell him. "Sometimes I read the books that used to belong to my dad. He wrote notes in the margin of some pages, and he circled certain words. It's kind of silly, but I pretend Dad's sending me secret messages."

Ol-Korrok doesn't laugh at me. He doesn't even crack a smile. He just puts his arm around me, and this time, having the wizard's hand on my shoulder feels kind of nice.

Finally, I ask him about his book. "What did you learn from all that reading you did in the Tower?"

He takes a deep breath and stops walking. For a moment, we both gaze in wonder at the swirl of stars all around us. Then the wizard says, "I learned that there's no shame in failure. Those who only succeed rarely learn the value of humility. My sister has never suffered a resounding defeat, and so she rules Palmara with total confidence that her way is the right way—indeed, the only way. She is proud, but she is wrong, Jax. She is wrong."

When I start walking again, Ol-Korrok doesn't join me. I look back and see he's pointing at something in the distance. I squint and see a small sun burning above a cluster of figures up ahead. My friends!

"Aren't you coming with us?" I ask, torn between wanting to linger with Ol-Korrok and the urge to race toward Vik, Kenny, Kavi, and the phoenix.

The wizard shakes his head. "This is as far as I dare to venture. Perhaps in time my sister will welcome me with open arms, but today is not that day."

I do my best to hide my disappointment. "I understand. Well, thanks for filling me in on the history between you two. When I was a witch's apprentice, Rule #1
was 'Always be ready.' With everything you've told me, I
feel more prepared to face Sis. Wish me luck!" I say with
a half-hearted grin.

The wizard steps forward and puts his hand on my
shoulder once more. With his other hand, he tilts my
chin so I have no choice but to hold my head up. "Luck is
for those with less talent. You are an extraordinary boy,
Jax. You see and hear things that others don't—much
like your mother before you."

My mother? Before I can ask how Mama fits into all
of this, Ol-Korrok continues. "But that's a story for another time. I want you to remember this: you were chosen for this mission because of your unique skills. But it
is your vision that most impressed me. You look into the
future and see a world that is healed and whole—just as
Source intended. I believe in you. Your friends believe in
you. Try to believe in yourself, too."

I barely have time to think of a response before the
wizard shape-shifts and in his crow form flies back
the way we've come. I watch him fly away, but within
seconds, he is swallowed by the darkness. Energized
by Ol-Korrok's kind words, I start walking toward my

friends. *I can do this,* I tell myself. I didn't succeed as Ma's apprentice, but maybe the wizard is right—maybe failing at one job makes me better qualified for another.

Suddenly, I hear Kenny's voice. "There he is! Jax—over here!"

They all start waving, and my heart fills with joy. I walk even faster, eager to share all that Ol-Korrok has told me. Then I break into a sprint and race along the enchanted bridge, ready for our mission to begin.

3

I'm running so fast I nearly knock my friends over when I finally reach them. Vik, Kenny, Kavi, and I are tight because we've been through *a lot* together. When Ma and I accidentally traveled back in time last spring, we wound up in the Jurassic period. Who did I turn to for help? Vik. Because he's my best friend and knows more about dinosaurs than anybody else—except maybe his little sister, Kavita. When we weren't looking, she found the three baby dragons in Ma's handbag and decided to keep one for herself. That was wrong and created all kinds of problems, but if Kavi hadn't been a dragon thief, Vik and I probably wouldn't have found out how cool Kenny is.

We all wound up in Esmeralda's Excellent Emporium of Exotic Spices, Magical Potions, and Mythical Creatures of All Kinds. That's where we inhaled the experimental gas that Blue had created. Now we've all developed traits that are the same as those of the magical creatures we met. Well, not all of us. Vik's still normal, but a few days ago, he handed over a phoenix egg he found in the community garden near his house. Vik had kept it hidden for more than a year! Then it hatched while I was in Chicago for the witch convention, and I kept it a secret from Ma. She was keeping secrets, too, because she didn't want me to testify against her friend Sis at the trial. But I did it anyway and got kicked out of the coven. Not for telling the truth. Turns out being a witch just wasn't my destiny.

It's a lot, right? All these adventures have definitely brought us closer together. I wouldn't have agreed to serve as ambassador to Palmara unless the Supreme Council allowed me to bring my friends along. And really, this new job only opened up because Sis refused to attend the trial. Blue accused her of holding a bunch of magical creatures against their will, and it's true. I know because I was there the night she took them away from Brooklyn—we all were. And now we're taking this bridge to the realm of magic because Sis sealed the gates that used to link our world to hers. She thinks the creatures from Palmara aren't safe around humans. My job is simple: I just have to change her mind.

"Where'd you go?" Vik asks when our group hug finally winds down.

"I was behind you the whole time," I tell him. "Ol-Korrok just wanted to talk to me in private."

"About what?"

The suspicion in my best friend's eyes makes me squirm a bit. I remind myself that I haven't done anything wrong and tell Vik the truth as we walk along the bridge. "The past. Ol-Korrok admitted that he made a mistake back in the day. He even said Sis was right to lock him up!"

"So he basically admitted he was untrustworthy?" Vik says.

I frown. "A thousand years is a long time, Vik. The wizard did his time, and now he wants to make amends. Everyone deserves a second chance, right?" I'm mostly talking about Ol-Korrok, but I'm kind of talking about myself, too. Vik reluctantly nods his head, and I breathe a silent sigh of relief. I understand why my friends might not trust the wizard, but I really want them to trust me.

Kenny nudges me with his elbow. "I wish you'd told us Ol-Korrok is part man, part crow. Remember what Jef told me? 'Beware the crow.'"

"I know—and you're right. I should have told you

that Ol-Korrok is a shape-shifter like Sis. But I don't think he's dangerous."

Vik snorts. "Really? Getting sucked through that silver bean felt pretty dangerous to me!"

"Well . . . Ol-Korrok apologized for that," I tell my friends. "He's still working on the enchanted bridge. It's brand-new, you know. I think we're the first people to cross it."

"Besides him, you mean." Vik must see the confusion on my face, because he offers me an explanation. "With all the gates closed, your wizard friend must have used the bridge himself to reach our world."

I hadn't thought of that, but Vik's right. I open my mouth to assure them all that Ol-Korrok isn't my friend, and then I realize that might not be entirely true. He and I do have some stuff in common after all. I decide not to say anything else about my conversation with the wizard for now. We need to focus on what lies ahead.

"Your phoenix sure seems to like it here," Kavi says, pointing at the glowing bird gliding above us on outstretched wings.

"I wonder if it's going to get any bigger." There's no way I could fit the phoenix in my pocket now. It's about the size of a bald eagle and looks less like a dainty hummingbird and more like a fierce raptor.

"We must be getting close to Palmara," Kenny speculates. "That might explain the phoenix's sudden growth spurt. It's almost home."

"Returning to its source," I say mostly to myself.

Suddenly, Vik stops walking and tilts his head to the side. "Does anyone else hear that weird music?" he asks.

We all pause on the bridge to listen, but the stars above us burn silently in the black sky.

"I don't hear anything," Kavi says before walking on.

"It sounds like a strange sort of harp or something," Vik insists, but when Kenny and I just shrug, Vik frowns and mutters something before trailing after his sister. I don't know why he's so grouchy, but I get the feeling it might not be wise to ask Vik what's up right now. I figure he'll tell me what's wrong when he's ready.

After we've been walking for a while, Vik points and says, "The sky is lighter up ahead. You can see that, can't you?"

The stars are definitely starting to thin, and those that are left look dim. The ebony sky has more of a deep purple tint that lightens in the distance to a soft mauve. I look ahead and think I can see a lone figure waving their arm over their head.

"Do you know that person?" Kavi asks.

"It must be L. Roy," I tell her. "He said Sis knew we

were coming and assigned him to the welcoming committee."

"A committee needs more than one person," Vik says sullenly.

"At least one person is happy to see us," Kenny says cheerfully. With Vik in such a sour mood, I'm grateful for my other friend's optimism.

"Aunty will be so glad we've come to visit," Kavi declares with confidence. "And Mo—I'm sure they've missed me as much as I've missed them."

"I bet Jef can give me some tips on how to fly straight," Kenny says. Then he grips his stomach and adds, "I hope the welcoming committee brought snacks. I'm hungry."

"Already? We just ate a little while ago," I remind him. Then I recall what the wizard said about time being elastic here. Maybe more time has passed than I realized. "Plus, you packed your own snacks, Kenny."

"I know," he says, "but I figure food must taste a whole lot better in the realm of magic."

I laugh. "The last time I was here, Ma shared her mango with me."

Kenny's eyes open wide. "Was it supersized or made of real gold?"

I shake my head, sorry to disappoint him. "Nope. It

was just a regular, juicy mango like the ones we eat back in Brooklyn."

Vik sighs impatiently and glares at us. "How can you be talking about *fruit* at a time like this?"

I take a deep breath so I don't lose my patience. "Relax, Vik. There's nothing to worry about. L. Roy will take us to Sis, and then we can make our case."

Vik scowls at me. "What if she refuses to listen to us? We're just a bunch of kids."

Kenny objects. "No, we're not—we're *enhanced* now, remember?"

Vik sneers at him and says, "You can barely levitate, Kenny. Do you really think you can stand up to someone as powerful as Sis?"

Kenny actually considers Vik's question for a few seconds before answering with a sincere shrug. I'm about to defend Kenny when Vik blurts out something entirely unexpected.

"Argh! Where is that strange music coming from?" Vik reaches up and grabs hold of his hair with both hands. "It's getting louder. You seriously can't hear it?"

Kenny and I shake our heads and exchange worried glances. What's going on with Vik today?

Vik clamps his hands over his ears and groans. "It's totally out of tune, and it feels like it's inside my head."

"It must be, because you're the only person who can hear it," Kavi says unsympathetically.

I pull my water bottle out of my backpack and offer it to Vik. "Here—have some water. Maybe you're just dehydrated."

"Maybe I'm not meant to be here," Vik says quietly after taking a few sips. "I just can't shake the feeling that something bad is about to happen."

I search for a way to reassure Vik. "Well, none of us can predict the future. But if something bad does happen—like, if Sis turns us away—then we'll just focus on finding my grandfather."

"And Aunty and Mo!" Kavita adds.

"And Jef," Kenny says with a smile. "I hope he can give me a tour of Palmara. I've been dreaming about this place ever since you told me about it, Jax. Think they have upside-down waterfalls or lakes full of chocolate?"

"I want to look for the unicorns!" Kavi says excitedly.

Vik and I exchange looks of surprise. I haven't seen enough of Palmara to know that there *aren't* any chocolate lakes, but that's definitely not why we're here.

As always, Vik is the voice of reason. "We don't have time for sightseeing. You two need to stop acting like tourists taking a vacation!"

"And you need to stop acting like such a grouch," Kavi

replies. "Why are you so angry? Here—have a marshmallow. Marshmallows always calm me down."

Vik snatches the spongy white cube from his sister's hand and flings it into the void beneath the bridge. "I don't need to calm down! I need all of you to start taking this mission seriously. Jax's grandfather is already missing, and we don't know what happened to him. We're heading into hostile territory. Just because you have special powers doesn't mean you're invincible!"

Kavi rolls her eyes and says, "Ignore my brother. He's just jealous because we're magical now and he's not. He's normal. Boring, annoying, and normal."

"Is that true, Vik?" I ask.

"I don't think you're boring or annoying," Kenny says, trying to be helpful.

"I meant the other part. Are you mad that you aren't . . . uh . . . hybrid like us?" I ask cautiously.

Vik shakes his head. It takes a while for him to find the words he needs. "I'm not mad," he says finally, glaring at his sister. "I just . . . I'm not like the rest of you. I'm not magical or special or . . . useful."

I can't hear Vik's weird music, but it's not hard to detect a hint of envy in my best friend's voice. I put my arm around Vik and give him an encouraging squeeze.

"You balance us out, Vik. We're struggling to manage these new skills, but you've always seen things clearly— just like a scientist. I'm really glad you're here with us."

Vik gives me a half grin and says, "Thanks, Jax. I know we've got a job to do, and I don't mean to be such a drag."

"We won't let anything happen to you, Vik," Kenny promises.

We all walk a bit faster now that the bridge's end is in sight. But after fifteen minutes of steady walking, we're no closer than before.

"Is it me, or are we not making any progress?" I ask.

"It feels like we're walking the wrong way on one of those moving sidewalks at the airport," Kavi says.

Vik sighs. "Great—a bridge that never ends. Did your wizard friend tell you *in private* how we're supposed to get off his amazing invention?"

I shake my head and look to L. Roy for help. Waving both arms, I yell, "L. Roy, we're stuck!"

I'm not sure my voice will travel that far, but L. Roy doesn't seem to have any trouble hearing me. He cups his mouth with one hand and shouts back, "You'll have to jump!"

Now that the sky is lighter, I can see that my

grandfather's friend is standing on the shore of a vast sea. Waves of black water gently lap against both sides of the bridge.

"So . . . who wants to go first?" I ask my friends. Then I think maybe *I* should go first. Isn't that what a leader would do? But before I can volunteer, Kenny speaks up.

"I think I can just fly over," Kenny says before lifting himself into the air. We watch as his legs pump the air as if Kenny's riding a bike. After just a few moments, he lands rather abruptly, accidentally splashing L. Roy.

"I'll go next," Kavi says.

Vik and I watch anxiously as she kneels like a runner about to start a race. A silent starter's gun must go off, because suddenly Kavi sprints along the bridge before jumping into the air. Vik gasps, and I feel my stomach drop—she leapt too soon! There's too much distance between where Kavi is now and where she needs to be. What happens if one of us falls into the black sea instead of landing on the shore? I can't see any sharks or even any fish swimming in the dark water, but there could be something even worse.

Then I hear Vik sigh with relief and watch in amazement as Kavi lands on the sandy shore in almost the exact same pose.

"She made it look so easy," Vik says nervously.

"Maybe it is," I tell him, hoping to relieve his anxiety even though my stomach is full of butterflies, too. "Maybe it's a mind-over-matter kind of situation."

Vik starts muttering something under his breath, like a mantra: "I think I can. I think I can. I think I can. . . ."

Vik flings himself into the air, but something goes wrong. Instead of traveling in an arc that starts on the bridge and ends on the shore, Vik begins to drift upward. He wheels toward the fading stars like an astronaut without a tether.

"Vik!" I cry, terrified for my friend. Then I look to L. Roy for help and realize he's already found a solution to the problem. I can't see anything in his hands, but L. Roy is tugging on something—and that invisible rope is drawing Vik closer and closer to the shore. After several anxious moments, Vik is close enough for Kenny and Kavi to grab hold of his feet and pull him down to the beach.

It's my turn now. Vik's mantra didn't seem to help him, but I decide to try one of my own. I repeat it over and over in my head with my gaze fixed on my friends waiting for me on the shore. *I believe in myself. I believe in myself. I believe in myself. . . .*

Just as I am about to start running, I feel pressure on

both my shoulders. Then my feet lift off the bridge, and golden light wraps me in a warm embrace. I glance up but can hardly bear to look directly at the brightly shining phoenix. It flaps its powerful wings just a couple of times, and we soar over the black sea, reaching the other side in a few seconds. The awe I see in my friends' faces matches the amazement I feel myself.

"Wow!" I utter breathlessly as the phoenix gently deposits me on the sand. The bird nuzzles my cheek with its beak before lifting up into the sky once more. I watch the magnificent creature circling overhead and marvel at the fact that just a few hours ago it was a tiny bird sleeping in my pocket!

"That was so cool!" Kavi cries.

Kenny beams at me. "Maybe in a week or two you'll be able to fly yourself, Jax."

I hadn't thought of that. I really don't understand enough about the phoenix's powers to know which traits will "transfer" to me. Then I look at Vik and see there's more fear than awe in his eyes. "What matters right now is that we made it to Palmara, safe and sound. All of us."

Kenny senses Vik's unease and backs me up. "Exactly. We make a great team! Right, Vik?"

"I guess," he says quietly.

Kavi slips her hand inside of his and says, "You were really brave up there."

Vik just shakes his head. "No, I wasn't. I was terrified." Then he turns to L. Roy and says, "Thanks for saving me, Professor."

L. Roy brushes Vik's gratitude aside with a wave of his hand. "No need to thank me, sonny. That kind of sturdy silk doesn't just appear out of nowhere. I daresay you've been marked."

Panic makes Vik's dark eyes grow large. "Marked?"

"Well . . . 'claimed' might be a better word," L. Roy says, as if that makes any more sense. Our confusion and Vik's growing terror prompts L. Roy to elaborate. "I never imagined I'd find a loose strand of silk all the way out here. I mean, either you're the luckiest kid in the world or . . ."

Vik swallows hard and asks, "Or what?"

"The spiders have claimed you as one of their own."

My mind races to find something reassuring to tell Vik, but he surprises me by staying calm. He looks at L. Roy and asks, "Do spiders make music here?"

This time it's the Professor's turn to look disturbed. "Why do you ask? This is very important, young man, so think carefully before you answer my next question.

34

Are you telling me you heard *a web song* out there on that bridge?"

"I don't know if it was a web song or not, but I definitely heard something out there. It sounded sort of like a funky harp."

"Kora!" L. Roy says excitedly. "Spiderwebs sing like the strings of a kora. This is incredible! The spiders have been dormant for decades. If I'm not mistaken, the last time anyone reported hearing a web song was back in 1993, when Trub brought—"

L. Roy's eyes suddenly find my face, and his excitement vanishes instantly. "Er, well, that's a story for another time."

I frown and decide not to be put off by L. Roy the way I was by Ol-Korrok. "That's the second time today someone from this realm has mentioned my mother."

"Really? How curious," L. Roy says as the rims of his ears burn red. "Well, we'd better be on our way."

"Who else was talking about your mom?" Kenny asks, ready to use his strength to defend my mother's honor.

"Ol-Korrok just said Mama could see and hear things that no one else could." I turn to L. Roy for confirmation even though I know I'm right. "That's who Trub brought to Palmara in 1993, right?"

"Well . . . yes," L. Roy says carefully.

"And did the spiders claim her, too?"

"Uh . . . I think you'd better save the rest of your questions for your grandfather. I'm sure Trub will be happy to share that chapter of your family history as soon as he returns from . . . wherever he is."

"Trub still hasn't turned up?" I ask.

L. Roy sees the worry in my face and gives my back a rousing thump. "Not to worry! I'm sure all will be revealed in time. Let me get my formal duties out of the way. Welcome to Palmara! You're right on time. How was your journey?"

"A little rougher than expected," I say.

"I see. Well, it may take a few moments for your legs to grow accustomed to solid land. There's no rush, so take your time. If you'll just follow me, I'll show you to your quarters."

L. Roy leads us away from the shore and along a dirt path that winds through a stretch of savanna. Kenny and Kavi have lots of questions, and the Professor happily obliges them. "Why don't we start with introductions?" he suggests cheerily. "I'm Professor L. Roy Jenkins, head of the Palmara welcoming committee, scientist, and all-around magic enthusiast. Jax and I have met before, but it's a pleasure to have so many young people in our realm. Children are rather rare in Palmara."

"I'm Kavita, and that's my brother, Vik," Kavi says, jerking a thumb over her shoulder without bothering to turn around.

"Fascinating!" L. Roy replies. "Two siblings—one marked by the spiders and the other bound to a particular dragon I know who happens to love sugary treats."

Kavi bounces up and down with excitement. "You've seen Mo? They're okay? Aunty, too?"

L. Roy chuckles. "Yes, yes, they're both well and eager to see you again. And I believe there's a certain fairy who's quite keen to see you again, young man."

That pleases Kenny so much that he lifts off the ground. L. Roy marvels at his flying ability and pulls a small notebook out of his back pocket. He's so busy observing the others and scribbling notes that the Professor doesn't pay any attention to me and Vik. We hang back, and for a while, we just walk in silence, absorbed in our own thoughts.

"I thought you said your mom hated it here," Vik says finally.

I nod uncertainly and try to recall the brief conversations I had with Mama and Trub about Palmara. "Trub told me Mama got frightened and just wanted to go home."

"Think it was the spiders that scared her off?"

I shrug. "She never mentioned seeing or hearing any spiders. It's kind of cool, really—being chosen like that. It means you're special, Vik."

"It's not cool if they chose me because I look especially tasty!" Vik counters.

"I'm sure the spiders here have better things to snack on. They sent that strand of silk to protect you. The spiders want you to stay safe—they're like bodyguards," I tell him.

Vik considers that idea for a moment and says, "My great-grandfather was an entomologist. He studied insects because he thought even the smallest creature could teach humans something important about life. And Aunty never let us kill bugs—not even nasty roaches! She used to say spiders were incredible weavers and their webs were like bridges reminding us that we're all connected."

"Makes sense," I say.

Our conversation ends when L. Roy turns and waves us on. "Come on, you two! We're almost there."

I hope the idea of having spider bodyguards makes Vik's bad feeling go away. I wish I'd gone to see Mama before leaving Brooklyn. I didn't know then what I know now, but maybe if I'd told my mother the truth about where I was going, she would have opened up about her time in Palmara. There's definitely a lot more I need to uncover. Trub will probably have some of the answers, and the rest I might have to figure out on my own or with my friends' help. I think Vik's aunt is right—everyone is connected somehow.

4

When my grandfather and I came to the realm of magic, we found Ma and Sis sitting under a tent. I didn't know then that Palmara had a capital, but the walled city up ahead is certainly impressive. Even from this distance, I can tell that the stone walls are high enough to keep out any unwanted visitors.

L. Roy has been chatting nonstop, and yet Kenny and Kavi manage to keep asking more questions. I haven't paid much attention to their conversation, but my ears perk up when I hear Kavi ask, "Isn't that Sis?"

I look up and see that she's pointing to a lone tall woman in a distant field. If we stay on the dirt path, we'll soon reach the stone city, but before I know what I'm doing, my feet turn into the field and I find myself wading through the tall grass toward Sis. My friends follow me despite the Professor's polite request for us to stay on the path.

I don't know why, but I imagined we would be presented to the Guardian of Palmara in some type of castle. Sis would be seated on a throne, and I would bow respectfully before making my case for the return of the magical creatures she took from Brooklyn. Instead, I find myself drawn through the field even though Sis has her back to me and seems just as indifferent to me as I am to L. Roy's cries.

"Jaxon, stop! My boy, please . . . you mustn't disturb . . . This really is highly irregular!"

I can tell that the Professor is hurrying to catch up with me. But I will reach Sis first, so he can't stop me from talking to her. Above me, the phoenix flies in tight circles. I don't know if the bird senses my racing heart, but its color shifts from golden yellow to fiery red. When I am just a few feet away from Sis, I open my mouth to speak, but she interrupts me by declaring in a stern voice, "I am busy."

I close my mouth and try to override my home training. Sis is an elder, and she basically just told me to leave her alone. But I have questions I need her to answer, so I say as respectfully as possible, "I'm sorry to interrupt you, but I need to find my grandfather."

Sis doesn't turn to face me. She doesn't acknowledge me at all! But after the fiery-red phoenix makes a few more laps around our heads, she whispers, "Be still." And the bird freezes mid-flight, hanging in the sky like a comet.

"Do you know what's happened to Trub? I think he might need help."

"I am busy, boy," she says in the same dull tone.

There is a basket hanging from the crook of her elbow. I watch as Sis plucks small orange berries from a shrub growing near her feet. Several turquoise dragon-flies zip and zag around her, almost seeming to point out ripe berries Sis has missed.

"What are you doing?" I ask, hoping my own curiosity might get her to take an interest in me, too.

"Gathering bilva berries."

"Do they taste good?" I see a shrub not far from me and stoop to pick some myself.

Finally, I have Sis's attention. She turns to watch me and just before I pop a juicy orange berry into my mouth says, "I wouldn't do that if I were you."

L. Roy is out of breath from chasing me across the field, but he still manages to chuckle as he slaps the berry out of my hand before it touches my lips. "My sincerest apologies, Guardian. I know my instructions were to show our young guests to their quarters, but—"

"*Guests* are invited," Sis says coldly.

L. Roy's ears turn red again. He tries to smile but just looks as uncomfortable as my friends and I feel. "Yes, of course. I meant to say that our *visitors* are anxious to speak with you but will wait until you have time to hear their petition."

"Their 'petition,' as you call it, is not my priority." Sis

turns once more to glare at me. "Surely you noticed the sleeping spell spreading across your realm."

I clear my throat and try to reply in a steady voice. "Of course—I helped Ma gather silver root to help folks stay awake."

Sis gives me a grudging nod. "That will only provide temporary relief. A more potent, permanent remedy is required."

"Like the vial you gave me when Ma couldn't stop sleeping?" I ask. Sis nods and turns to leave, but I call after her. "How will you get the cure to Ma? You've sealed all the gates connecting the two realms."

Sis turns slowly and glares at me. "I did. And yet, here you are."

L. Roy chuckles nervously and pulls my arm until I'm standing behind him. He's not much taller than me, but I appreciate having him as a shield against Sis's quiet rage. "Where there's a will, there's a way, hey? Heh-heh. We won't keep you any longer, Guardian."

"See that I'm not disturbed, Professor, and remember that your patients require your full attention."

"Of course," he replies, making a show of herding us back toward the dirt path.

"Now go," Sis says softly, and instantly the phoenix is released from her spell.

L. Roy tries to steer me out of the field, but I brush his hand off my elbow. I am not ready to be dismissed. I'm not sure where my confidence is coming from, but I make a U-turn and stride across the field until I am standing right next to Sis.

"Your brother told me he has forgiven you for banishing him," I tell her.

Sis's lip curls in disdain. "And you believe him?"

I nod. "You took away most of his power. He has no reason to lie."

To my surprise, Sis lifts her head and laughs at the sky. "My brother does not need a reason to lie. He deceives others because it pleases him to sow confusion and chaos wherever he goes."

I frown and suddenly feel the urge to defend the wizard. "Maybe that's the brother you remember, but that's not who Ol-Korrok is now. He's changed."

For a moment, I think Sis is going to laugh again. Then her face hardens, and she snarls at me instead. I watch for other signs that she's about to transform into a dragon, but the Guardian remains in her human form. "My brother cannot change. Didn't he tell you? I took from him the power to shape-shift. He will only ever be a selfish, miserable liar."

"He can still turn into a crow," I remind her.

"Yes. He can manage that but no more. You are only a child, so I do not blame you for swallowing his tall tales and honey-coated lies. My brother has had a thousand years to perfect his performance, and he found in you and your friends an ideal audience. You are trusting and gullible and unable to see the villain behind the veil."

Gullible? With my cheeks burning, I say, "We didn't come here to talk about your brother. We're here on behalf of the Supreme Council."

"You may tell yourself that, boy, but make no mistake—you are doing his bidding."

"We want you to open the gates and restore the travel and trade routes that once connected the two realms."

"What you want is no concern of mine," Sis says. "I do not serve you or the Supreme Council. Ol-Korrok is a charlatan, yet you believe every word that drips from his oiled tongue. You do not trust me, though I offer nothing but the truth. Perhaps I should hold my own trial. Would you like that, boy? For my first witness, I could call . . . your grandfather."

"Trub's here?" I ask excitedly.

Sis shakes her head and offers me a smile that is both cunning and concerned. "He has disappeared. But you know that already. Isn't that why you convinced your friends to join you on this journey?"

"L. Roy told us you sent Trub on a mission."

Sis nods. "And no doubt the Professor also told you that your grandfather failed. My brother escaped the Tower in which he was locked and found a way to cross into your world. I should not have trusted a mere mortal with such an important task."

I frown. "Trub is an expert when it comes to locks."

"The Forgotten Tower cannot be opened with any ordinary key. Only very advanced magic could have opened that particular lock."

"What are you saying?" I ask defensively. "My grandfather wouldn't have let Ol-Korrok out if you told him not to."

"Wouldn't he?" Sis asks, but her question is more like an accusation. "My brother can be very persuasive. He easily convinced *you* to help him."

My head feels like it's spinning. It feels like I can't defend Trub without accepting blame myself. But I haven't done anything wrong—and neither has Trub. "Something must have happened to him," I say.

"I have no doubt whatsoever that something *did* happen to your grandfather."

I wait for Sis to share what she knows, but she offers me nothing but silence. Exasperated, I finally blurt out, "Well, what happened to him?"

"You should have asked my brother that when you had the chance," she replies coolly.

The annoyed look on my face seems to amuse Sis. Eventually, she sighs with boredom and tells me the little she does know. "I sent Trub to the Forgotten Tower to ensure that the lock still held. But instead of securing the prisoner, your grandfather obviously set him free. Trub is wise not to show his face around here. I don't know what my brother promised him in exchange for his help, but there is a high price to be paid for betraying *me*."

I'm relieved when L. Roy suddenly finds the courage to defend his friend. "Trub has always been loyal to you, Guardian."

"Did you not hear what the boy said a moment ago, Professor? Apparently, *people change*." The sarcasm in Sis's voice makes my blood boil, and the phoenix once again turns from gold to red.

I'm so wrapped up in my concern for Trub that I forget my friends are worried about their family member, too. Vik clears his throat to draw Sis's attention. "We'd like to see our aunt," Vik says respectfully.

"And Mo!" Kavi adds with a hint of attitude.

Sis studies the siblings for a moment, her gaze lingering longer on Kavi. I wonder if the Guardian can sense the girl's new dragon traits. "Those I retrieved from Brooklyn are still under quarantine," Sis tells them. "Until their condition is fully understood, I cannot permit them to come in contact with the others."

"What about Jef? Is he okay?" Kenny asks anxiously.

He blushes as Sis also considers Kenny closely for a moment. I can't tell if she is weighing his concern or searching for similarities between Kenny and her fairy servant. Either way, Sis surprises us all by answering his question with a sharp snap of her long, elegant fingers. Instantly, several dragonflies zoom around Sis's face before speeding off in different directions.

"I have notified your friends of your arrival. You will have plenty of time to become reacquainted once you have settled in. Now go."

I don't know why I feel the urge to press her when it's clear we've been dismissed. "What about the Supreme Council? They sent me here to tell you that—"

Sis stops me with a wave of her hand. "I will hear your petition along with all the others at the usual time," she says before turning back to berry picking.

L. Roy volunteers the answer to the question I was about to ask. "Noon on the third day."

I accept the information with a nod and this time allow L. Roy to herd us back to the path. While my friends babble excitedly about the upcoming reunion, I think about the challenge ahead of me: I have three days to find my grandfather.

5

The dirt path widens as it leads us out of the grassy fields and up a steep hill. A twenty-foot wall circles the stone city, which, L. Roy informs us, is the unofficial capital of Palmara. When Kavi asks what the city is called, the Professor smiles and says, "Kumba. Home.

"Every effort was made to decentralize power," he explains in that frustrating way that often leaves us more confused. "You'll notice that the city's design is quite deliberately democratic. No one is elevated above anyone else."

As we pass through the wide gate, I look up and find no guards stationed atop the thick stone walls. This city may try to make everyone feel equal, and the open doors are welcoming, but it still feels like a fortress. If those heavy wooden doors were ever shut and barred, it would be hard for anyone other than a giant to force their way in. Vik must be thinking the same thing because he nudges me with his elbow and asks, "Are there giants in Palmara?"

"Probably," I tell him. "But if Sis lives in this city, then any giants around here probably work for her."

Vik accepts my answer with a nod, and we follow the others inside the walled city. I soon understand what L. Roy meant about the layout of the city. Instead of a square courtyard where people can gather, we walk into a sort of semicircular, open-air lobby. Leading into the shadows are six alleys with ten-foot walls made of the same gray stones. We follow the Professor as he guides us down a cool, dim cobbled lane that winds like a river. Occasionally, we pass a wooden door studded with brass nails or painted in colorful geometric designs. Some entryways have no door, and as we pass, I glimpse a compound containing several small round huts and folks gathered around a fire. Through partially opened doors, I see gardens overflowing with unfamiliar vegetables and trees heavy with fruit. My stomach grumbles, and I realize that I am hungry. But I've already decided to skip dinner. As soon as I can, I'm going to slip away and figure out how to reach the Forgotten Tower.

Eventually, we reach an opening in the wall that leads to a compound with four huts. "I think you'll be quite comfortable here," L. Roy says with obvious satisfaction. "I chose quarters that aren't too far from the restricted area."

"Is that where Aunty is?" Vik asks.

"Yes, though technically she is no longer under quarantine. She's become quite indispensable, really—her bedside manner with the ailing creatures is remarkable."

Kavi frowns. "Which creatures are ailing?"

"Fear not, my dear. Mo is positively thriving. It's the other two dragons who, by comparison, are not developing as expected. And those who returned from Brooklyn with Sis . . . well . . . we can save that conversation for later. Why don't you freshen up and I'll return to collect you in about an hour? We've prepared a special feast to welcome you to Palmara."

While my friends claim the huts they want, I slip out of the compound and hurry after L. Roy. "Professor, wait!" My voice ricochets off the passage's high walls. "Could I ask you something?"

He turns and glances at the watch on his wrist before grinning at me. "Of course, my boy. How can I help you?"

I take a deep breath and say, "I need to know how to get to the Forgotten Tower."

L. Roy frowns. "I'm afraid I can't help you there. That

ancient prison was forgotten in part because all maps showing its location were destroyed."

"By Sis?" I ask.

The Professor nods but hurries to add, "She preserved the master, of course. But I believe she entrusted that original map to Trub before he set out. Along with the key to the Tower."

"Did you see the map before he left? Do you remember anything that might help me find him?" I don't bother to hide my desperation.

L. Roy thinks for a moment before clapping his hands so loudly that the sound echoes up and down the narrow alley. I glance over my shoulder to make sure none of my friends is within earshot. I know they'd help me if I asked, but I feel like this is something I should do on my own. Before we parted, Ma told me to figure out what would help most and do that. Enjoying a magical feast with my friends won't help my grandfather—and it won't bring me any closer to solving the mystery of my mother's time in Palmara.

"As it happens," the Professor says excitedly, reaching into his back pocket, "I made a hasty sketch in my notebook. I'd never seen such an interesting antique map! The writing was largely indecipherable—a language no longer spoken here in Palmara—but the landmarks were clear." He leans in and confides, "Of course, Sis doesn't allow copies to be made of her personal possessions, but the historian in me simply couldn't resist."

"I thought you were a scientist," I say, impatiently waiting for L. Roy to flip through the many pages of his little book. All are covered in illegible notes, strange diagrams, and peculiar symbols—along with evidence of the food he happened to be eating at the time. Some pages are stuck together, and a few loose ones even fall out and drift to the ground. I gather the loose sheets of paper and hold them while L. Roy keeps searching for the map.

"Cartography falls somewhere between the two, really, being a representation of actual terrain as well as a record of trade routes and settlements." Just as I'm starting to feel lost again, L. Roy exclaims, "Ah—here it is!" before proudly revealing a dog-eared page covered in scribbles, doodles, and what look like coffee stains. "The Forgotten Tower is here," he says, pointing to a large X near the top right corner. Then he dabs at a sticky orange smear next to the X, licks his fingertip, and declares, "Guava jam, I believe."

I take a moment to examine the rest of the sketch. Along the margin there are waves that seem to represent a body of water, though there are spirals mixed in

with the waves. Beside those are stacked triangles that might be mountains, and a thick river winds through them that looks more like a snake. There are other shapes below the triangles that might be flames, and in the bottom corner are half a dozen flies buzzing by a creature that looks a bit like an alligator.

I'm frustrated by the lack of names and suspect a

three-year-old could have drawn a better map. I point to a line of double-headed arrows just beneath the X and ask, "Are these supposed to be trees?"

L. Roy responds with a grave nod. "Technically, the Forest of Needles has no trees—just stone spikes that are sharp enough to shred human flesh. The only creatures to be found there are a peculiar species of lemur and . . ." The notebook remains open, but something in the Professor's face seems to close.

"And?" I prompt, hoping he'll go on. If I'm going to make this journey by myself, I'm going to need as much information as possible.

It takes L. Roy a moment longer to decide just what he wants to tell me. Finally, he tugs his long mustache and says, "Well, Jax, when places are forgotten, facts are often replaced with rumors and speculation. Having never been to the forest myself, I cannot verify the truth of such stories. But darkness is the source of all life, and the deepest places are the darkest. Over time, most creatures find their way into the light—but not all. Some prefer to linger where they are less likely to be disturbed."

Frustrated, I forget about whatever it is that lives with the lemurs and try to ask a question that will get me a straight answer. "So the Tower lies beyond the

Forest of Needles. And how do I get to the forest from here?"

"You'd need to take a boat up the coast of the Black Sea—just like Trub did. But you can't manage such a trip on your own, my boy. You'd need a guide and supplies, clothing suitable for multiple climates. Best to get a good night's rest, and in the morning, we can put our heads together and figure out a viable plan." Seeing the disappointment in my eyes, L. Roy adds, "You never know—if we wait a few more days, Trub may find his own way back. It'd be a shame if you weren't here to greet him when he returns."

L. Roy gives my arm a squeeze and turns to go, but I don't want that kind of empty assurance. I grab his hand instead and plead, "Can I take a photo of your sketch?" My phone doesn't have service here in Palmara, but the camera still works. L. Roy studies me for a moment before holding his notebook open while I zoom in on the confusing map.

When I get back to our compound, I find my friends standing around a small fountain. Kenny is practically ladling water into his mouth with both hands. "Ah," he sighs. "This is the best water I've ever had. My mother's always trying to get me to drink eight glasses a day. I could drink eight gallons of this stuff! Come and try it, Jax."

I force myself to smile and pull my water bottle out of my bag. It's a good opportunity to refill and get ready for the journey ahead.

"We saved that hut for you," Kavi says, pointing to the one farthest from the fountain but closest to the doorway that leads to the passageway.

"Thanks," I say, and fill my bottle with the crystal-clear water. I take one sip and realize Kenny is right. "Wow—this *is* good."

"Right? I bet dinner is going to be *amazing*! Whatever's on the menu, I'm going to have two helpings," he says.

"What if it's something gross?" Vik asks.

"Nothing could be grosser than my mother's 'healthy' cooking," Kenny replies. "The other night she made a pizza with no meat or cheese!"

Kavi laughs before wandering over to a tree that has been trained to grow up the compound wall. Its fruit looks a bit like plums, though the smell is closer to cherries. I pluck a few that seem ripe and slip them into my bag. The phoenix must approve, because it takes bites of ripe fruit growing at the top of the tree.

I fake a yawn and tell my friends I'm going to take a quick nap. Kavi and Kenny are too busy picking fruit to respond, but Vik comes over and asks, "You okay, Jax?"

I nod a bit too eagerly and head over to the hut they left for me. "Just tired. I'll be fine by dinner," I call over my shoulder. My plan is to pretend to sleep so soundly that my friends leave for dinner without me.

Vik looks suspicious, but after a few seconds, he says, "Same here. Think I'll lie down for a while, too."

We both pull aside the piece of cloth that serves as the door of our huts. Inside I find a low cot and a table that has a basin, a towel, and bar of soap. Not luxurious but bigger and nicer than the closet I had to sleep in at Miss Ellabelle's Home for Working Women and Girls back in Chicago. I take off my shoes and ease myself onto the cot. I actually am kind of tired, but I don't have time for sleep right now. I need to come up with a plan. Traveling at night shouldn't be a problem since I basically have a flying torch for a pet!

I have a sketch of a map that I can barely read. That means I'll need to get directions from a local. So far I haven't seen too many people in the stone city, but it shouldn't be too hard to find someone willing to help. The way L. Roy tells it, the locals here are excited about our arrival. Once I know where I'm going, then I just have to find the courage to strike out on my own. I'll have the phoenix and whatever power is stirring inside of me. That along with the feeling in my gut that Trub needs me will have to be enough.

Before long, I hear L. Roy's voice in the compound. To my surprise, no one enters my hut to witness my excellent deep-sleep performance. Instead, I hear Vik telling the others to go on without us.

"I'll wait till Jax wakes up, and then we'll come find you."

L. Roy gives Vik directions to the dining hall, where the feast is taking place. Then the compound grows quiet, and I swing my legs over the edge of the cot. I'm not sure why, but I feel pretty angry at my friend's interference. Before I can smother my anger, Vik pulls back the curtain to my hut and says, "The coast is clear."

"What are you doing?" I hiss, not even bothering to hide my irritation.

"What any good friend would do," Vik replies calmly as he hefts his backpack onto his shoulder. "You're running away—and I'm going with you."

"You can't, Vik."

"Of course I can. This was the plan all along, right? Kenny and Kavi would stay here with Sis while you and I went looking for your grandfather."

He's right. That is what we decided back in Brooklyn. "Trub isn't your family—or your responsibility, Vik. Don't you want to see your aunt?" I ask.

Vik just shrugs and bites into one of the ripe red fruits from the tree in our compound. "Sure, but Aunty will still be here when we get back. We've got three days before you have to face the dragon lady, right? That should be plenty of time to find your grandfather."

All of a sudden, I understand why I am so angry. Maybe being bound to the phoenix means developing a fiery temper. Problem is, I can't tell my best friend that I might be able to travel faster without him. I can't fly yet, but when the phoenix perches on my shoulder, I definitely feel a surge of energy. It runs through my entire body, making me think it won't be long before I'm able to lift myself off the ground. Or maybe the extra energy will help me run super fast—I really don't know. L. Roy said the shared traits would most likely emerge in moments of crisis. I hope Vik and I can avoid any dangerous situations, but if we do run into trouble, will I be able to save my best friend *and* myself?

"Come on," he says impatiently. "We better get going. This city is like a maze. It might take us half the night just to find our way back to the front gate!"

I grab my bag and follow Vik out of the compound. The open sky overhead is blue, but I think that means night is falling. We wander the shadowy passages without passing anyone.

"Everyone must already be at the feast," I conclude dejectedly.

Vik nudges my shoulder with his own and says, "Then I guess that guy's not hungry."

Up ahead is a tall figure wearing a dark cloak. He would blend into the shadows entirely except for one thing: his eyes are on fire! When I first met Vonn back in Chicago, he wore mirrored sunglasses that hid the fiery pupils of his eyes. This man has the hood of his cloak pulled low over his head, but the familiar orange glow is unmistakable. He doesn't appear to be doing anything. He's just . . . watching us. That final clue gives me the courage I need to approach the man and ask for help. With Vik close behind me, I rush up to him and say, "Excuse me, sir. I—I don't mean to be rude, but . . . uh . . . are you a . . . ? Or do you happen to know . . . ?"

When his burning eyes gaze into my own, all the words I need to say seem to dissolve on my tongue. For a moment, I stand before the tall figure, transfixed. Finally, he pulls his hood down farther to hide his eyes, and I feel my question taking shape once more.

"I don't mean to be rude, but . . . you remind me of someone I know. A friend. His name is Vonn. He's a Watcher back in Chicago."

The alley is dim, but I still see a small smile form on the man's dark face. "I have not seen my brother Vonn in many years."

"Vonn's your brother?" I ask, amazed but also hopeful that this will make the stranger more willing to help us.

"Every Watcher in this world is a brother of mine," he replies. "Vonn is one of the youngest among us. Is he well?"

Vonn looks like a teenager, but he's actually hundreds of years old! If this man is his big brother, then he must be ancient. I nod in response but for the sake of honesty add, "Vonn's okay, but he's pretty busy. There's a lot going on back home right now."

The figure tilts his head sideways, which I think might mean "What else is new?" I find myself missing the warm glow of his eyes, but feeling Vik's finger poking me in the ribs helps me remember that I need to ask this Watcher for help. "I'm Jaxon, and this is my friend Vik, and . . ."

"I am Jamor."

"Nice to meet you, Jamor. Actually, it's *way* better than nice. I'm *so* glad we found you." For a second, it occurs to me that, as a Watcher, Jamor might have spotted us long before we spotted him. "Vik and I are trying to reach the Forgotten Tower, but we don't have a map, just this sketch."

I hold out my phone to show the picture I took of L. Roy's notebook. "Can you tell us how to find this river?"

Jamor briefly examines the photo, his fiery eyes lingering on the river that snakes between the mountains.

"That is not a river, friend. That is Imfezi. The cobra."

Vik's astonishment matches my own, but he's the first to speak. "There's a giant snake in the middle of Palmara?"

Jamor gives us another sideways nod. "Not anymore. What remains is a tunnel—a fossil of sorts. A memory etched in stone."

Relief spreads across Vik's face. "It's dead! That kind of cobra I can handle."

"It is not without risk," Jamor warns, "but the Imfezi is the safest of the routes available to you."

"I wonder why Trub didn't go that way to reach the Forgotten Tower," I say mostly to myself.

"I witnessed his departure," Jamor tells me. "Your grandfather set sail with a captain known for his ability to navigate the treacherous whirlpools of the Black Sea. That is the fastest route, but also the most dangerous." He pauses to point a long finger at the image on the screen. "Your other options are to cross the Scorched Sands or to wade through the Abysmal Swamp."

Vik blinks and says, "I vote for the cobra tunnel."

"A wise choice," Jamor says, "though, as I said before, the Imfezi is not without hazards of its own."

"Such as?"

Jamor looks up at the sky and then motions for us to follow him. "We should go before we lose the light."

"Oh—I forgot to mention our other traveling companion." I sense the phoenix before I see it, but I'm glad I didn't glance up at the sky because then I would have missed the expression on Jamor's face when the phoenix flew down to settle on my shoulder.

"You are blessed, indeed!" he exclaims. "Did my brother Vonn witness this marvelous creature?"

I nod. "It was tiny then—just a newborn. Being here in Palmara seems to have brought on a growth spurt."

"Naturally," Jamor says with another tilt of his head. "All things grow stronger when they return to their source. Let us proceed."

6

Vik subtly gives me the thumbs-up, and I grin back. We follow Jamor down the dark, winding passage that finally leads us to another impressive gate. I figure we must be at the back of the enclosed city, because instead of grassy fields, we pass through a village of round huts. There are a few goats grazing while tied to posts, but all the homes seem to be empty.

"Everyone's at the welcome party except us," Vik says with a hint of longing.

"It's not too late to change your mind," I tell him.

He shakes his head and points to two more cloaked figures up ahead. They seem to be waiting for Jamor, and he greets them by touching his forehead to theirs. Not bothering with introductions, Jamor simply says, "I will take these friends as far as the Imfezi." The other Watchers nod, and Jamor walks alongside them as they move toward three horse-drawn wagons tied to the low branches of a nearby tree.

"Are there usually so many of you in one place?" I ask as Jamor unties his horse's reins.

"Usually, no. But something is stirring," Jamor says quietly. His brothers nod but calmly prepare to depart. The lack of panic in their manner and movements reassures me somehow. The two other Watchers wave to us before steering their horses in opposite directions.

"So . . . you three are going to investigate?" Vik asks.

Jamor shakes his head solemnly. "We are Watchers. Our role is only to observe."

As he climbs up to the driver's seat, Vik gives me a funny look. I can tell he expects me to say something, but it's not my place to tell these Watchers what to do. They have their job, and we have ours. Jamor extends his hand to help us climb up and settle next to him.

Vik clearly isn't as willing to let it go. "This thing that's stirring—is it dangerous?"

Jamor urges his horse forward with a light slap of the reins. He tilts his head in that mildly frustrating way and says, "Imbalance always brings risk to those who crave stability."

"So that means everyone's at risk, since no one in their right mind wants things to be unstable."

A crow caws loudly, drawing our attention upward. Vik and I exchange a wary glance. Jamor doesn't seem bothered by the bird, his gaze tracking the phoenix instead as it loops in the sky above.

"Instability creates opportunity . . . for some," he says.

Vik squirms on the wooden bench. I can tell he wants to start a debate with the Watcher. I pinch his thigh, but Vik just swats my hand away and dives in. "So as a Watcher, if you saw something terrible happening, you wouldn't intervene? In our world, bystanders are people who let bad things happen instead of standing up for what's right."

I can't believe Vik is being so rude when Jamor is helping us *right now*! I give an uncomfortable laugh and try to clean up the mess Vik is making. "I think my friend is just a little confused. What he means is—"

"I understand his meaning perfectly," Jamor says in a gentle voice. If Vik's comment has insulted him, it doesn't show. "In your world, there are people whose role is not unlike my own. I believe you call them journalists."

I roll my lips together so Vik won't see the smirk that's itching to spread across my face. Jamor doesn't look smug at all as he defends his own profession by reminding Vik of another.

"In times of war, these journalists bear witness. They take photographs and interview those most affected by the conflict. They do not take up arms to engage in battle. They do not choose one side over another. Instead, they observe and report everything they have seen. In this way, a record is created that is objective and fair to all."

Vik considers Jamor's points and admits the Watcher is right. "That's true. But here in Palmara, we're not at war . . . are we?"

I expect Jamor to shake his head or at least give us another sideways tilt. But for several seconds, he sits frozen beside us. I recall Jamor's words from before and feel a chill run up my spine. *Something is stirring. . . .*

"How long will it take to reach the tunnel?" I ask.

"We should arrive by dawn," Jamor replies. Then he tilts his cloaked head back and says, "You're welcome to make yourselves comfortable. Sleep if you can, for tomorrow's journey will be challenging. You will need to have your wits about you."

Vik and I decide to take Jamor's advice and climb into the back of the wagon. With a sack of flour for a pillow and an extra cloak for a blanket, we stare up at the countless stars. The phoenix streaks by like a comet but returns a moment later and nestles between us. I don't know how much time has passed since we crossed the enchanted bridge, but I do feel weary—mostly from worrying about all the questions I can't yet answer.

Vik nudges me and says, "It's fainter than before, but I can still hear it."

"The spiders?" I ask.

Vik nods, no longer worried that he alone can hear the web songs of distant spiders. "I think we're meant to be here, Jax. I'm glad I came along. I know I was kind of freaking out before, but now . . ."

I just stare at the glittering sky and wait for Vik to finish his thought. Then I hear him snoring faintly and realize he has fallen asleep. Before long, the rocking of the wagon lulls me to sleep, too.

I wake up and rub my eyes to clear my double vision. Then I remember I am in Palmara, where anything's possible. That must be why there are two suns shining in the purple sky. Vik is already up and sitting across a small campfire from Jamor. Something sizzling in his frying pan smells a bit like bacon, so I go over to join them.

"Sorry I slept so long," I say.

"You slept well," Jamor says with a smile. "Journeys can be tiring. Let us eat together before we part ways. I was telling your friend that sunlight does not easily penetrate the tunnel, so it is best to make a start while the suns are high in the sky."

The crisp green strips don't taste anything like bacon, but they're flavorful and filling. After breakfast, Jamor tells us a funny story about Vonn. When it ends, we thank Jamor for all his help and wave as he heads down the road, leaving us alone at the mouth of the tunnel. At one time, it probably looked like the yawning jaws of a cobra, but today it's hard to see the resemblance. Two stalactites that look like a snake's fangs have broken off, making the stone creature much less menacing. Frilly vines spill out of the snake's eyes and trail to the ground. Through the veil of leaves, we can see shafts of light coming from holes in the roof of the tunnel.

Vik pulls aside the curtain of vines and peers inside. "Doesn't look that bad, right? Smells kind of funky, but I guess snakes aren't known for having fresh breath."

I chuckle and look for the phoenix. I find it a few yards away and call to it but get no response. Finally, I go over and touch the golden bird on its head. "Ready?" I ask.

The bird raises its eyes to mine and slowly shakes

its head. Then it reaches over its shoulder and plucks one of its beautiful tail feathers. The phoenix offers it to me, and I take the peacock-like feather from its beak. "What's this for? You're coming with us, aren't you?"

The bird sadly shakes its head once more and then lifts into the sky and flies away.

"Was it something I said?" Vik asks. "Maybe birds and snakes just don't mix."

I'm not sure what to feel. The phoenix doesn't belong to me, but I didn't expect it to abandon me at the start of our journey. I examine the feather for a moment and somehow know that this gift is meant to help us. I take a deep breath and step over the pile of rubble that was once the cobra's lower fangs. "Let's do this!"

My voice echoes faintly inside the tunnel. The first thing we notice are the bones. Either a whole bunch of animals came here to die or some ravenous creature has been using the tunnel as its lair. It must have been a long time ago, though, because most of the bones are draped in cobwebs. Vik spends fifteen minutes trying to identify each victim. None looks human, which is a relief. When Vik bends down to examine a large horned skull, a small, shiny black spider descends from above and lands on his backpack. My instinct is to swat it away, but now that Vik has been "claimed," I'm not sure that's a good idea. So instead I say, "There's a spider on your back. Want me to brush it off?"

Vik glances over his shoulder and just shrugs as if to say, "Whatever," before going back to the strange skull. "This looks kind of like a narwhal—or a giant unicorn. Is that even possible?"

"In Palmara, anything's possible," I reply.

As we move farther into the tunnel, the bones disappear. The sunlight from above starts to diminish as well, and before long, we hear the faint trickle of running water.

"There must be a spring nearby," Vik speculates. He kicks a loose stone into the stream and takes the flashlight out of his backpack. Vik turns it on and scans the tunnel, alarming several bats hanging from the roof. They're larger than the bats I've seen in our world—and they're white! Their red eyes flash with alarm as they swoop past us. We both duck, and Vik points his flashlight at the ground as we move forward.

"We're heading downhill," I remark. It's clear from the dropping temperature in the tunnel that we're heading deeper underground.

The stream running alongside the path becomes wider and deeper. When Vik kicks another stone into the water, something flashes beneath the surface.

"Did you see that?" he asks warily.

I nod and peer into the fast-flowing river. "Probably just a fish," I say uncertainly. But as we continue, blue lights swim beneath the water's surface. When Vik picks up a stick and touches its tip to the river, several mouths suddenly appear and fight to sink their razor-sharp teeth into the wood! Vik yanks the branch out of the water, bringing with it a fish that looks a lot like a giant piranha. It flops frantically on the stony path before launching itself back into the river.

"Whoa," Vik says, breathing hard and pressing himself against the tunnel wall. "We are *definitely* not going for a swim."

Avoiding the river is easier said than done, however, because as it widens, the path narrows, and before long, it becomes difficult to walk. We inch our way forward, hugging the wall of the tunnel, but finally, we're forced to stop and come up with another plan. Vik cautiously scans the tunnel with his flashlight and spots what looks like a canoe a little farther ahead.

"Think it's seaworthy?" he asks dubiously.

"It better be," I reply, "otherwise we'll be lunch for those vicious fish."

We draw closer and inspect the canoe as best we can with limited light.

"Look—your feather's glowing!"

Vik's right. The tip of the phoenix's tail feather is glowing red, like an iron pulled from the fire. When I hold it over the water, the blue lights under the surface seem to scatter.

"Fascinating," Vik says. "Something about the phoenix's energy alarms those fish. At least those blue lights make them easy to spot. Creatures that live deep in the ocean sometimes generate their own light."

"Bioluminescence," I say, recalling our lesson from science class. "Some fish use the light to lure prey."

"Exactly. But we are smart enough not to fall for that trick." Vik puts one foot inside the canoe and stomps hard. "Traveling by boat will be faster. Think we should risk it?"

I hold up the feather and examine the shrinking path ahead. "I don't think we have much choice. Plus, someone clearly left this boat here, so maybe that's what travelers are supposed to do."

Vik puts his other foot inside the canoe, and we both hear the wood creak under his weight. "Something tells me this boat hasn't been used recently," he says as he lowers himself into a sitting position near the front of the canoe.

I give the hunk of wood a shove before quickly

climbing in and seating myself behind Vik. We don't have a paddle, but the current carries us along rather quickly. I hold the feather like a fishing pole, and it serves to ward off the unfriendly fish.

"This isn't so bad," Vik says, leaning back to make himself more comfortable. "We'll reach the end of the tunnel in no time at this rate."

Just as I let myself relax, I feel something cold on my legs. Water is seeping into the canoe! "Uh—Vik . . . ?"

He turns to look at me but keeps pointing the flashlight ahead of us. So I'm the first one to see the foam forming on the water as it crashes against the sharp rocks jutting out of the river. Our comfortable log ride suddenly turns into a speeding, sloshing, soaking adventure.

Over the roar of the current, I yell, "We've got to stop the leak!" At this point, my legs are partly submerged, and cupping water in my palms does nothing to help. As soon as I bail some water out of the canoe, more splashes in as the canoe bobs uncontrollably.

"Can you feel where the hole is?" Vik hollers over his shoulder.

I feel the bottom of the canoe and find the leak on the right side. When my finger accidentally pokes through the hole in the wood, one of the fish seizes the opportunity to chomp down. I manage not to cry out but swing the feather over to that side of the boat to keep the piranhas away.

"Did you find it?" Vik asks.

I nod and take his hand, leading it to the region that needs repair. I expect Vik will take something from his backpack and try to plug the hole, but instead he just stares at his left hand for a long time.

This is no time to worry about a splinter in his finger! "What are you doing?" I shout over the roar of the river.

Vik takes a deep breath and calmly replies, "I think I can make a web."

It's so loud in the tunnel that I'm not sure I heard him correctly. But I watch in awe as Vik presses his fingertips together and then slowly draws them apart. Somehow, he's spinning silk!

When he's made enough web to cover the hole in the canoe, Vik stretches the sticky substance and presses it against the weakened wood. I continue to bail water as best I can, and Vik manages to keep the canoe from smashing against the rocks. Suddenly, the current slows and the noise in the tunnel diminishes. Vik and I are both breathing heavily. We look around, relieved and amazed that we survived the journey.

"We made it!" Vik cries, flashing me a triumphant grin.

Then the canoe starts to turn slowly in the water. Before long, I am sitting where Vik was just a moment ago. My end of the boat sinks deeper into the water even though our weight is distributed evenly. I look up at Vik and see the triumph in his face turn to confusion and then panic as the canoe spins faster and faster. Finally, we realize our canoe is caught in a whirlpool!

"What do we do now?" I ask frantically.

Once again, Vik stays calm. He tilts his head as if he's listening to something far away. Then he says, "Whatever you do, don't let go of my hand."

The boat is turning faster and faster, but Vik pulls himself up and shines his flashlight at the ceiling of the tunnel. There are no white bats hanging upside down, but there is a small triangle of light.

"I don't think the tunnel has an exit," Vik explains. "We're going to have to climb up and out."

I nod even though it's hard to see how we could do that when our boat is being sucked into a river filled with flesh-eating fish. If the phoenix were here, it could lift us to safety using its powerful wings and talons. But all I have right now is a floppy tail feather. L. Roy said my inherited powers would reveal themselves in moments of crisis, but I can't think of a way to save us despite our dire circumstances.

The canoe is tilting more steeply. Vik pockets his flashlight and manages to climb to the highest part. Then he reaches back for my hand. I unsteadily get to my feet and try climbing upward, though I slip several times. Maybe Vik has web on the soles of his feet, because he isn't sliding at all. His hand is glued to mine by sticky strands of spiderweb.

"On the count of three, we jump," Vik says. The certainty in his eyes doesn't make my heart stop racing, but I trust my friend and do as I'm told. As soon as he yells "Three!" we leap into the air, traveling much farther than I ever thought possible. Vik slaps his free hand against the wall of the tunnel, and the same sticky substance on his palm keeps us from falling into the river.

The problem is, what do we do now? Vik can't let go of me, and he can't let go of the wall. I look down and see blue lights gathering in the water just a couple of feet from my shoes. I wave the glowing phoenix feather, hoping to ward off the fish, but they no longer seem scared. One even jumps out of the water and sinks its sharp teeth into the rubber sole of my sneaker! I shake my leg and send it flying back into the river, but other fish start leaping and snapping at me.

"Hold still, Jax!" Vik hollers.

"I can't," I tell him. "These fish are trying to eat me!"

I know I have to do something. I feel a dangerous mix of emotions bubbling inside of me. Fear, anger, and panic but also . . . determination. *I got us into this situation, and I am going to get us out,* I think to myself. I hold the tail feather up toward the triangle of light streaming through the hole in the ceiling. The tip is still glowing red, but as I focus on it, warmth and light spread from the end of the feather to the quill that I'm holding in my hand. It spreads up my arm and throughout my entire body.

Vik must feel it, too, because he turns and asks, "What are you doing?"

"I'm not sure," I admit, "but I think the phoenix part of me is finally waking up."

It's great that my special powers have been activated, but now I have to figure out what I can *do* with all the energy inside of me. I hear a voice so soft that its words are hard to distinguish: *press . . . pressure . . . compress . . . concentrate.* Is the phoenix somehow communicating with me from outside the tunnel?

Focus, Jax.

I know that voice. It isn't the phoenix guiding me—it's Ma! Into the cauldron boiling inside me I add a few more emotions: joy, gratitude, and relief. Next, I imagine that I can reach into the cauldron with my bare hands and scoop up the red-hot soup. It immediately hardens in my palms, making it easy for me to shape my feelings into something compact. I press my feelings together like I am forming a snowball, and instead of feeling hot, I start to feel *strong.*

"I need you to let go," I tell Vik, but he just shakes his head at me. I try again, hoping my calm voice will encourage him to trust me. "It's okay, Vik—really. You can let go of my hand."

"And feed you to those vicious fish? No way!" Vik replies. But I can see the strain in his face. He can't hold on to both me and the wall much longer.

The heat coming from my body causes the silk strands binding our hands together to fray. But even when the sticky substance is gone, Vik continues to clutch my hand.

"Let go, Vik," I say once more. "It's okay—really." To prove it, I close my eyes and think about the triangle of light above us. I don't have wings like the phoenix, but I feel my body rising toward the ceiling. Vik watches,

amazed, and gradually he loosens his grip on my hand. Soon I am above him, and he has no choice but to let go. I wish I were strong enough to bring Vik with me, but I just keep my focus, trusting that my friend will use his own special skills to climb up the wall until we both reach the hole in the roof.

Not that long ago, what I wanted most was to learn how to be a witch. I thought casting spells would be cool, but then I found out that wasn't my destiny, and I agreed to become ambassador to Palmara. Now I'm not really sure what I am . . . but it feels great! This must be what Blue had in mind when he tested that experimental gas on me and my friends. It has made us more independent, more resourceful. We don't need adults to do everything for us anymore.

Before long, I see the two suns shining in the mauve sky. With freedom in sight, I pull myself out of the tunnel and then reach back to help Vik climb out as well. For a while, we just sit there in the sunlight, breathing heavily and then laughing as the adrenaline starts to wear off.

"Wow, Vik—were you bitten by a radioactive spider? You looked like Miles Morales down there!"

Vik gives me a playful shove, but I can tell he appreciates the comparison. He examines his hands for a moment before shrugging. "I don't know how to explain it, but I'm glad I finally have a way to contribute. I was starting to worry I'd just be a burden to you."

My face burns, and I pretend to search for a granola bar at the bottom of my backpack so Vik can't see how guilty I look. "*You* saved *me*," I remind my friend—and myself. "Thanks, Vik."

"That's what friends are for," he replies softly, but I see the pride in his eyes.

"Guess we don't need this anymore," I say, dropping the phoenix's feather into the hole we just crawled through. It drifts back down to the river, and we hear an electrifying crackle as it lands on the surface of the river. Soon the smell of fried fish wafts up to us, making my stomach growl.

"What a day! Let's have dinner," Vik suggests with a smile. I agree, and we pool the food we brought. As the suns set, Vik and I reminisce about our exciting day before falling asleep under the stars.

7

I sense her long before I see her. First, my heart beats more quickly, and then it swells within my chest. I stand up on my hind legs and sniff the air, but it is not her scent that confirms she is near. There is no doubt in my mind—I feel in my bones that my dragon kin has arrived. We do not share the same blood, for we were born to different species, but the girl called Kavita is somehow bound to me—and I to her.

Just as my siblings suffered while we were apart, I have felt incomplete without Kavi in Palmara. Perhaps it is the same for Sis and her brother. There were already rumors of his escape, but Kavi and the boy called Kenny bring confirmation that Ol-Korrok has indeed left the Forgotten Tower and reached the human realm. We don't learn about the outcome of the trial before the Supreme Council until the following day, however, because no one wants to discuss serious matters at the feast. So many sweet things are on the menu, plus the children have brought marshmallows! But the fullness I feel this evening isn't from all the treats I put in my belly. Having Aunty and Kavi and my siblings all together helps me understand a new word I learned just last week: *family.*

If you have never attended a feast in Palmara, then you have missed out on an extraordinary experience. We welcome our guests in humble ways—there is no excess or extravagance—but our hospitality is heartfelt. To be seated at the round table in Kumba's Great Hall is to be drawn into our community not as an outsider, but as an equal. The hall is not as full as it would be ordinarily. Tonight only those Palmarans who are under quarantine are permitted to dine with our human visitors. Like me, they are eager to hear news of the other realm, and the hall buzzes with anticipation.

Though the children have never visited Palmara before, the magical bond they share with its residents makes this feel like not only a reunion but also a homecoming. Kavi's eyes shine with awe as we show her into the Great Hall, but I also sense recognition. Without speaking, she lets me know that there is a feeling of familiarity in this place.

Seated between me and Aunty, she says aloud, "Why do I feel so at home here? Palmara is nothing like Brooklyn!"

"Home isn't a place—it's a feeling," Kenny says, taking the seat next to Aunty and helping himself to one of the freshly baked rolls in a basket on the table. Jef zips around the room like a dragonfly but finally settles on Kenny's shoulder. The Professor takes the seat next to the boy, and my siblings, as always, stay as close to me as they can. Lex curls up on my lap, and Rex sits on the floor but leans against my leg.

Kenny takes a long drink from the glass of water next to his plate. "Why is water so delicious here? I wouldn't mind drinking eight glasses a day of this stuff!" He burps, blushes, and says, "Excuse me!" before finishing his thoughts on home. "You always hear grown-ups saying, 'Home is where the heart is.' I always thought it was kind of corny, but it's actually true. That's why you can feel at home in a new place even if you're from somewhere else. You just have to be with people you love."

I understand him perfectly. Not only because my English is improving every day, but because his words ring true. My siblings and I were born in Brooklyn, but only I had the opportunity to spend time in the human world. Though we are the same age, my brother, Rex, and sister, Lex, are much smaller than I am. They also act very young—always needing attention and clinging to me as if I were their parent. Perhaps they are afraid that we will be separated again. Perhaps they can tell that when I go to sleep at night, I dream about returning to Brooklyn.

The Professor says Lex and Rex failed to thrive in the first weeks of their life because they were separated from me and yearned to be back in the place of their birth. Can you miss a place you don't really know? They only got a glimpse of Brooklyn when Kavi took us out of the mint tin in Ma's bag. But I guess it was enough because my siblings endlessly ask about the human realm and never tire of hearing about my one ride on the subway.

My siblings struggle to describe the unhappy feeling that plagues them. I speak dragon-tongue, English, and Gujarati, but I, too, find it hard to explain how I feel sometimes. I am a dragon, but I'm not like the others. I live in Palmara, but a part of me wishes I were still in Brooklyn. I enjoy the company of humans, like Aunty and the Professor, yet I have much in common with the other magical creatures. Kavi says she reached the realm of magic by crossing an enchanted bridge designed by Ol-Korrok. I think maybe that is what I am—the thing that links two worlds. Something in between, neither here nor there, this nor that.

I forget all about these mixed-up emotions during the feast. The fairies serve platter after platter of Palmaran delicacies that look kind of strange but taste delicious. While we wait for dessert to be served, Kenny agrees to show us his newly acquired magical skills. Kenny is much bigger than the average fairy, and he isn't as elegant or agile as Jef. But he manages to lift himself up to the rafters and slowly circles the room before toppling his empty chair with a rather abrupt landing. Kenny is determined to improve and gratefully accepts advice. It is clear that Jef is proud of his friend despite Kenny's imperfect flying skills. Rex and Lex can only speak dragon-tongue, but they urge me to share their best tip with the boy.

"Keep your butt up," I tell Kenny. "My siblings say that helps."

His freckled cheeks turn pink, but Kenny still smiles as he thanks us. Kavi giggles behind her hand, but Jef gives a nod of approval. "I'll have to give that a try," Kenny says.

It isn't clear yet which dragon traits Kavi has inherited. Leaning close to me, she confides that her temper gets the better of her at times, and that seems to be the only time her strength appears. I don't expect Kavi to get angry during the feast—but I am wrong.

Vikram and the boy named Jax are missing from the Great Hall. The Professor assures us they probably got lost while exploring the stone city, but he is wearing a false smile beneath his bushy mustache. He does not reveal the secret he knows about the two boys, but Kavi suspects the truth: they have gone on an adventure without her. "It isn't fair!" she fumes, pounding her fist on the table. "They didn't even let us know where they were going."

Kenny just shrugs and serves himself another slice of creamy banana cake. "Well, we knew Jax really wanted to find his grandfather. I guess he decided not to wait till tomorrow and Vik probably offered to go with him."

"*I* would have offered, too. *I'm* a lot stronger than Vikram—*he* doesn't even have any special skills."

"And you do?" Aunty says with a disapproving arch of her eyebrow. If there's one thing I have learned about Kavi's great-aunt, it's that she doesn't like a show-off. "What special skills do *you* possess?" the elderly woman demands of her cocky young niece.

Kavi falters and glances at me, but I don't know how to help her. In a much quieter voice, she says, "I can turn into a dragon."

Kenny stops sucking icing off his fingers to correct her. "Not exactly. I mean, your eyes definitely look like Mo's, but . . . you're still just a girl."

Kavi presses her lips together and glares at Kenny. She blinks once, and her eyes suddenly do look like mine! Then smoke starts to come out of her nostrils. But when Kavi opens her mouth, she doesn't breathe fire. I sigh with relief and wonder if I can help her learn to control her new powers even though I'm still learning how to control my own.

Kavi stands up so fast that her chair tips over. With her hands on her hips she declares, "I am not 'just a girl'!"

Kenny looks a little scared and holds up his hands to indicate he's ready to surrender. "I only meant that you're not a dragon. Not really. Just like I'm not a real fairy. I'm still a boy."

Aunty intervenes before Kavi can say or do anything else. "Kavita Patel, you will not make a spectacle of yourself this evening. You are a guest here at Kumba and must respect your hosts. Pick up your chair and apologize for your terrible manners this instant. *Tut-tut-tut.* Imagine what your mother would say if she could see you now."

Kavi sulks but does as she's told. When she is seated at the table, I try to talk privately with her. Aunty speaks dragon-tongue, too, but I think I can direct my thoughts to Kavi only.

"Don't be upset," I say silently, putting an arm around her shoulder. "It will take time to understand your abilities."

Kavi's eyes open wide, and I see that they are human once more. She inches her chair closer to mine even though we don't need to be near one another to communicate. "Do *you* think I'm a dragon? I'm definitely more than *just a girl.*"

"I think we are something entirely new and unique. Some people may find us...confusing. Try to be patient with them—and with yourself."

Though the others find her menacing, I know that Kavi wouldn't hurt anyone. I think she just wants to be seen as someone who is important and capable. Kavi hates being dismissed, and people do seem to underestimate how clever she is. Her big brother seems to cast a large shadow, and like everyone else, Kavi wants to stand in her own light. I wonder if my siblings ever feel that way.

Kavi laughs as much as the others for the rest of the evening, but I sense that she is feeling anxious about her brother. And because she is troubled, I feel uneasy as well. Aunty tries to assure Kavi that Vikram can take care of himself, but I see the worry that tugs at the corners of the elderly woman's mouth, making her smile not entirely convincing. This is what it means to be part of a family. Your problems are not your own, because everything is shared. I cannot simply enjoy the party and ignore the anxiety unsettling my kin.

When Kavi first met my siblings, I could tell she was surprised by how different we look. Not only am I much bigger than Lex and Rex, but their scales are no longer purple like mine. My siblings look like twins, with their matching blue scales and orange wings. Yet Aunty explained to me that there are many kinds of families, and so it doesn't bother me that the members of my family don't all look the same. Seated around the table with plenty of food to eat and room for everyone to sit comfortably, I feel safe—accepted, valued. I hope everyone here feels the same and knows they, too, are wanted and welcome.

When everyone has eaten their fill, talk around the table turns to the feud between Sis and Ol-Korrok. Kavi and Kenny share some troubling news about the human world. Mention of Blue seems to make the quarantined creatures more dissatisfied with their confinement, and they vigorously defend their friend.

"Blue has always been misunderstood!" an indignant pixie exclaims.

A sleek black panther growls in agreement and adds, "Those who don't know him judge him unfairly."

"He tried to steal Mo!" Kavi cries. "Was that fair?"

"Ssssssteal?" hisses a large serpent. "Blue merely invited your friend to join us in his magical tattoo menagerie."

I don't recall ever receiving an invitation from Blue but decide to stay silent for the time being.

"Blue was just looking for a way to allow us to stay in the human world," explains a soft-spoken faun.

"He was our protector!" the pixie insists.

"And though we are in exile, he continues to act in our best interest—unlike the Guardian," says a furry, frowning troll.

"How is it in your best interest for Blue to cast a sleeping spell over all the adults in two of our biggest cities?" Kenny asks.

"I'm sure it's just a temporary measure," the panther replies.

"And harmlessss!" hisses the serpent. "Who couldn't use a few more hours of sleep anyway?"

Kenny frowns. "That's not the point—"

"There's a reason the Supreme Council sent four children to Palmara instead of four adults," says a rather large owl. "Sometimes age is not an asset."

"I agree—children have not had time to adopt the biases and prejudices of their parents," the pixie says solemnly.

Kenny opens his mouth to object but seems to decide against it. Kavi assures the others that Jax will do his best to convince Sis to reopen the gates she sealed. She turns to me and silently communicates, "Then you can come back to Brooklyn and visit me whenever you want!"

"I'd like that," I tell her before our attention is drawn back to the other quarantined creatures.

The pixie hovers next to Kenny and says, "Tell your friend to tell Sis that we miss having access to the human realm. Tell her we belong to both realms now. This illness—if indeed that's what it is—comes from the cruel separation from our human friends that the Guardian imposed upon us."

"Why don't you tell her yourself?" Kenny suggests.

"How?" asks the faun. "We're confined to our compound until it's clear we're not contagious."

"The Professor can give you the all clear—can't you?" Kavi asks.

L. Roy coughs uncomfortably as everyone turns to him. "Well, I . . . ahem . . . I suppose that would be all right, since there's no indication that the general population would be at risk."

"Come to the assembly," Kenny says. "Have your say."

"Let the Guardian know how you feel," Kavi adds. "Sis might ignore a couple of human kids, but she can't ignore the citizens she's meant to serve."

"What have you got to lose?"

Kenny's question hangs in the air until the Professor clears his throat rather loudly. When he has everyone's attention, he announces, "We've kept our guests up long enough. Let's conclude this evening's festivities and allow them to get a good night's rest. I'm sure this conversation will continue over the coming days." He rises from the table, which seems to be the cue for everyone else to do the same.

The magical creatures file out of the Great Hall, some stopping to shake hands with the children. I follow Kavi and Kenny out and overhear some of their whispered exchange.

"What will we do if Jax and Vik don't come back? What if something's happened to them?"

From the look of surprise on Kenny's face, it's clear he hadn't even considered that possibility. "I'm sure they're okay, Kavi. They only left a few hours ago," he reminds her. "Plus, they do have a phoenix with them, and your brother's a really smart kid."

"I guess," she says doubtfully. Then Kavi takes a deep breath and with more confidence says, "You're probably right. Vik and Jax always look out for each other. But . . . what if everything *is* okay and they still don't get back to the capital in time—what will we do then?"

Kenny thinks for a moment. "Jax is the official ambassador, but we're his friends. If he can't do the job he was sent to do, then it's up to us, right?"

Kavi nods at him before glancing at me over her shoulder. Torches fill the alley with orange light, but I see something like a shadow lurking in Kavi's dark eyes. Doubt, perhaps.

When we finally say good night and head off to our respective rooms, I lie awake for a while, thinking of a way to help Kavi. I cannot leave Kumba to search for her brother because I am still under quarantine. And if I tried to slip away, Lex and Rex would want to come with me, which would make the journey more difficult. I guess that's why Vik left Kavi behind. Before I drift off to sleep, I come up with a plan that will increase Kavi's confidence without requiring us to leave Kumba.

The next day, I ask Kavi if she'd like to take a walk with me. I hoped we could have some time on our own, but as soon as I stir from my bed, my siblings do the same. When I share my plan with the Professor, he gives us permission to go no farther than a mile from the stone city. I lead Kavi into the fields, and my brother and sister fly above us, playing tag as if they're both on an invisible leash that I hold in my hand. After about a mile, the grass thins and we find ourselves in a secluded area surrounded by a tall outcrop of rocks.

"This is what you wanted to show me?" Kavi asks skeptically. "It doesn't look very . . . magical."

I smother a smile, sorry to disappoint my friend but also amused by her assumptions about magic. "How do you know these rocks aren't magical? They could be enchanted—or cursed."

Kavi's eyes open wide. "Really?" She examines the rocks with new interest and respect.

"Everything magical isn't covered in fairy dust. If you

only look at things that glitter, you'll likely miss many mundane but magical things." Kavi nods to show that she understands. I think she's going to be a good student. I hope I can be a good teacher!

"I brought you here because I thought this would be a good place for you to train."

"Train?"

"You want to learn how to breathe fire, don't you?"

Kavi nods eagerly. Yet despite her obvious excitement, her next question reveals her fear: "What if Aunty finds out?"

"Your aunt believes self-discipline is very important. I think she would want you to learn how to control your new abilities—don't you?"

Kavi nods slowly, and the doubt soon leaves her face. "You're right, Mo. I need to prove to Aunty that I'm responsible and not reckless. I'm not a danger to anyone—not out here, at least."

"Exactly. Now, I've noticed that your internal fire seems to be triggered whenever you feel upset. But you need to be able to summon it without getting angry. Otherwise, you'll lose control, and that *is* dangerous."

"How do I do that?" Kavi asks. "Can you show me?"

The wind has blown a twig up against the rocks.

I focus, open my mouth, and direct a thin, spiraling stream of fire toward the twig. It burns to ash in an instant, but nothing around it is scorched by flame.

Kavi applauds my demonstration and says, "That was amazing! You were so . . . so . . . precise. Just like a surgeon. I want to do that, too!"

I smile, pleased by her admiration. I almost wish Sis were here to see how well humans and magical creatures work together. I am ready to help Kavi, and it was Aunty who taught me to be aware of my power. Creatures who have fire inside of them cannot afford to be careless. A simple sneeze could have disastrous consequences! Aunty told me that everyone learns differently. Because I like sugary things, Aunty would reward me with a treat every time I learned a new lesson. Kavi likes sweet things, too, but I decide to try a different approach.

"Why did you get mad when Kenny said you weren't a real dragon?"

Kavi scowls and folds her arms across her chest. "That's not all he said. Kenny told everyone I was 'just a girl.'"

"You *are* a girl, aren't you?"

Kavi's face smooths itself out. "Well—yeah. But that's not the point."

"What *is* the point? Explain it to me."

"Some boys think they're better than girls," Kavi tells me. "They're always trying to act tough, and they won't let girls join in when they're playing a game or building something cool."

"Is Kenny one of those boys?" I ask, knowing full well that he's not.

"N-no," Kavi admits. "He's usually really nice to me."

"Then why did you get so angry last night?" Kavi just shrugs, but I can tell she's starting to feel frustrated. I keep on pushing to see if I can make her explode. "Do you think you're right all the time?"

"No! Nobody's right *all* the time. But I am right *most* of the time. And if someone says something that's wrong or untrue, I'm allowed to correct them."

I'm glad Aunty isn't here to hear her niece's remarks. "Do you like it when other people correct you? That's what Kenny was trying to do, and you snapped at him."

"No, I didn't."

"Yes, you did. He held up his hands like this because he felt like he was under attack." I hold up my claws as Kenny did the night before.

Kavi turns away and folds her arms across her chest. "I didn't attack him! Kenny is just . . . too sensitive."

"Like you."

Kavi spins around. She blinks at me, and her brown human eyes shift to orange dragon eyes. "I am not too sensitive," she says with a soft growl.

"Are you sure?" I shrug and answer the question myself: "Maybe you're right. Maybe you're just weak."

That does it! Smoke curls from Kavi's nostrils. She folds her hands into fists, takes a step closer, and glares up at me. "I am NOT weak. I am STRONG!"

I nod and wait for Kavi to figure out what I'm doing. After a few seconds, she steps back and opens her hands. Kavi looks at the ground, embarrassed by her near eruption. "You did that on purpose, didn't you?"

"Yes. Tell me what you felt inside when you started to get mad."

She thinks for a moment and then says, "Hot—I always feel really hot before I . . . change." Kavi wipes the sweat off her brow with the back of her hand.

"What else? Do you feel anything in your chest?"

"A . . . a . . . tickle. No—it's more like an itch that I can't quite scratch."

"Hmm. Maybe you aren't generating fire because you don't have a clear focus. That can make it hard to aim your flame. Think about what Kenny said last night. I need you to tell me exactly why it hurt your feelings."

Kavi presses her lips together and thinks for a long

while. Then she takes a deep breath and says, "What 'just a girl' really means is I'm not as good as a boy. It means no one's going to give me a chance to try something new or prove what I can do. If I really am 'just a girl,' then there's nothing I can do. I can't change who I am, and I can't change their mind about me. It's like . . . being locked in a cage when I want—I *deserve*—to be free."

There are tears shining in Kavi's eyes. I have learned this about humans: sometimes they act angry when, really, they are in pain. "I want you to close your eyes." Kavi does as I ask, and two tears roll down her cheeks. "Think about that cage you just told me about. Can you see it?" Kavi nods. "Now focus on the door of the cage. It's locked and you want to get out. Imagine that you have a key in your pocket—a key made of fire. You have to put the key in the lock and turn it until the door opens. Think you can do that?"

"I'll try."

I watch as Kavi's forehead creases with concentration. Two tendrils of smoke rise from her flared nostrils, but when she shapes her mouth into a little O, nothing comes out. Kavi clenches her fists and opens her mouth even wider, but it doesn't help. Finally, she lets out a frustrated shriek that draws the attention of Lex and Rex. They quickly descend and protectively wind their bodies around mine.

Kavi opens her dragon eyes and gasps. She holds out her hands, stunned by the long, curved claws that have replaced her short human fingernails. "What am I doing wrong?" she asks with fresh tears in her human eyes.

I gently fold Kavi in my arms and give her a long hug. Lex and Rex follow my lead and rub up against her legs, purring like cats. "You have to be patient—it takes time to learn a new skill, but you can do it," I assure her.

"How long did it take you?" she asks.

Kavi and I met just a few hours after I was born. She knows I've been breathing fire my whole life. "It was different for me. Don't try to be like me—or any other dragon. You're unique, so you need to figure out what works for *you*."

Kavi sniffs and says, "In almost all the movies I've seen, dragons are scary. They breathe fire to get rid of humans—usually the ones who are trying to steal their gold."

"I don't have any gold," I tell her. "And I wouldn't want to hurt anyone with my fire."

"Then, why do you have it?" she asks.

I've never thought of that. "It's just . . . part of who I am," I reply.

Kavi bends down to pat my siblings on the head. "Can your brother and sister breathe fire?"

"No—but Lex and Rex can fly, and I can't." As if I have just reminded them of their ability, my siblings launch themselves into the sky once more.

"Do they ever play by themselves?" Kavi asks.

I shake my head and try to smile. I don't want it to seem like I don't love my siblings, because I do.

"So you basically have to babysit them *all* the time. That's got to be annoying," Kavi says quietly even though there's no chance of Lex and Rex hearing her.

I lower my voice as well. "It was hard for them when we were separated. I think they feel safer when we're together. They don't want to lose me again."

Kavi watches them circling us in the sky above. She frowns and surprises me by saying, "I'm sorry I took you away from your family. It was selfish of me. You were just so cute and affectionate, and I wanted to have something all my own. Something special that I wouldn't have to share with Vikram."

"I understand. I'm glad I had the chance to see the human world, even if it was just for a little while."

With her eyes still on my siblings, Kavi sighs and says, "I think my brother wishes I would disappear for a while. He thinks I'm a pest—and I can be sometimes.

But I'm going to try to be a better sister—and a better dragon!"

"That means keeping your fire power under control. Ready to try again?" I ask.

Kavi nods and closes her eyes. "Ready."

"This time I want you to imagine something different. There's a banner strung across these rocks. It's made of paper, and someone has painted five words in bright red paint. Can you see the banner in your mind's eye?"

"I see it," Kavi replies. "But what does it say?"

I take a few steps back. When I'm at a safe distance,

I tell Kavi the five words that are guaranteed to light a fire inside her: *KAVI IS JUST A GIRL.*

Even without being able to see her face, I know that Kavi's dragon eyes are open. She holds her arm rigid, leans forward, and blows a hot blast of fire at the imaginary banner. The flames scorch the bare rocks, blackening them instantly.

"I did it! I did it!" Kavi cries triumphantly.

I let her bounce up and down for a while before stepping close once more. "How did that feel?"

"It felt AMAZING! Let's do it again!"

So we do. Each time, I give Kavi something smaller

to envision. It takes several hours, but eventually, she learns to summon her fire and direct it where she wants it to go.

"I can't wait to show Aunty," Kavi says as we head back to the stone city. "She'll be so proud of me."

"I'm impressed, too," I tell Kavi. "I didn't expect you to learn so quickly."

Kavi gives me a bashful grin. I think to myself that Aunty might be prouder of her niece's modesty. For a while, we walk in silence, but I sense that Kavi has something more to say. I wait for her to open up, but it is not until Kumba is within sight that Kavi touches my arm. I stop walking and turn to face her. "You're worried about your brother," I say, anticipating her next words.

Kavi nods and looks up the hill at the wall encircling the capital. "He's out there somewhere ... without any way of defending himself."

"Palmara is not without danger, but my kind would not attack a human unless they were provoked. Vik isn't likely to place himself in that sort of situation, is he?"

"No. But if Jaxon got himself into trouble and needed help ..." Kavi blinks back tears and takes a deep breath. "I just wish I was there to protect my brother. Because now, thanks to you, Mo, I really could keep him safe. I'm really glad you taught me how to breathe fire. I think I'm going to need my dragon skills soon." She pauses for a moment to watch Lex and Rex soaring overhead. "Will they grow as big as you?" Kavi asks.

I look up at my siblings and smile as they frolic in the sky. "Eventually."

"And will you all grow to be as powerful as Sis?"

I frown. I know of only one dragon that could equal Sis, but she stripped her brother of his power before banishing him from the capital. "Why do you ask? What's troubling you, Kavi?"

She turns away from Kumba and looks across the rippling fields of grass. "I don't know how to explain it. It's like there's something—or someone—standing just behind me. I know that they're there, but I can't quite see them. And whenever I turn my head, they disappear."

"This person follows you?"

"It feels that way. It's like having a sometimey shadow that isn't mine," Kavi says before offering a weak laugh. "Silly, right?"

"Not at all. This could be very serious. We should tell Aunty and the Professor."

Kavi nods, and we continue along the path that leads to the stone city.

"We're almost home," I say with a smile, hoping to lift Kavi's spirits.

But she doesn't smile back. Instead, Kavi says, "I don't think I'll be going home anytime soon."

8

Vik and I fell asleep feeling pretty good about our triumph in the tunnel, but our sense of accomplishment doesn't last all that long. The next morning, our journey continues as we follow a dusty path that winds through desertlike terrain. Cactuses menace us with their prickly spines, but they can't compare to the danger that awaits us.

I've heard Ma say that some folks can't see the forest for the trees. Well, there aren't many trees out here in the desert. I guess I had an image in my mind of a regular forest and that's why I didn't recognize the wall of glittering rock. Towering above us and stretching to the left and right as far as the eye can see is the Forest of Needles. I'm not sure what I expected. I mean, the name alone could inspire nightmares. And L. Roy did tell me not to expect any trees. But the stone spikes he mentioned are massive—not skinny like actual needles—and the "forest" is so dense that it's hard to imagine lemurs or any other creatures living here.

I gaze up at the sheer cliff face and try not to look as discouraged as I feel.

"So . . . ," Vik says with forced optimism. "What's the plan?"

I hear a familiar screech overhead and look up to find the phoenix soaring above the blades of stone. Vik saved me yesterday, and yet I feel a familiar itch of irritation. I'm not powerful enough to lift myself over the daggerlike rocks, but the phoenix could probably carry me across the forest. Vik has some spider skills now, but will they get him to the other side?

"Depending on how big it is, I can try flying over the forest with the phoenix. Any chance you can shoot silk like Spider-Man?"

"I don't think so," Vik says doubtfully. He reaches out and tentatively touches the cliff. "Ow! It feels like a really deep paper cut." Vik squeezes his finger as he checks for stone splinters and a pearl of blood appears. He wipes it on his jeans and says, "Maybe I can wrap my hands in silk and climb the needles that way."

We both know that won't work. I remind myself to stop thinking about what's most convenient for me and to consider what other folks might need. Vik is part of the team, and there's no *i* in *team*. There's no *i* in *lemur*, either, but the furry white creatures must find us interesting, because their heads start to appear from behind the stone shards.

I've seen lemurs on TV and in a zoo, so I'm not surprised by their small black faces and long, curly tails. I like the way lemurs leap on their long legs, and their honey-colored eyes always seem full of curiosity. Lemurs never seem scary to me, not even when they're part of a troop. But the lemurs watching us from within the Forest of Needles are different in one significant way: they're huge! I have never seen a cute, furry lemur that's as big as a gorilla!

I must look a little scared, because Vik whispers, "Most lemurs are vegetarians," to reassure me. Then he pulls a piece of fruit from his bag and tosses it to the lemur closest to us. When the creature greedily catches the fruit and samples its sweet flesh, Vik calls out, "Hello! Can you tell us how to cross the Forest of Needles?"

The smallest lemur in the troop clings to its parent's back. It makes a sound that's close to a giggle and points at something farther down the cliff face. Vik and I walk in that direction and soon discover a very narrow staircase of sorts. The steps are really just hunks of stone that have been worn down by centuries of rainfall and people's feet. The stairway is so tight that we have to walk single file, and after climbing for several minutes, Vik and I reach a small alcove situated between three towering spires of stone.

The lemurs soon join us, leaping from needle to needle, their rubbery palms and soles protecting them from the razor-sharp rocks. I pull another piece of fruit from my backpack and offer it to the baby lemur. It checks with its parent before climbing off their back and entering the alcove.

"Is there a path that leads to the other side of the forest?" I ask after handing over the fruit. The lemurs don't need a path, but if there's a staircase, then I'm guessing humans and other creatures come here often.

The little lemur sniffs the fruit before taking a giant bite. Red juice stains its white fur, but the lemur enjoys its snack too much to care. When it's done eating, it looks at me expectantly.

"Uh . . . I don't have any more fruit." I turn to Vik and ask, "How about you?"

Vik shakes his head, and the little lemur does the same. "Is it copying you or answering my question?"

Vik shrugs, and the little lemur mimics him once

more. "Great. Maybe we should try talking to the grown-ups."

The little lemur surprises me by tugging at my jeans. "Shifaka," it says softly.

"I didn't get that—did you?"

Vik cups his ear and leans forward, hoping to encourage the young lemur to repeat himself. Instead, the furry creature points up at a large and rather plump lemur before repeating, "Shifaka."

Then the little lemur scurries back to its mother, and the rest of the troop moves off. The large lemur named Shifaka climbs down a huge stone spike. It can't fit inside the alcove, but it seems willing to talk.

"Hi!" I start with a friendly wave. "I'm Jaxon, and this is my friend Vik. We need to reach the Forgotten Tower. Do you know how we can cross the Forest of Needles?" The phoenix screeches as if to chastise me for not including it in my introductions. I point at it and explain, "My phoenix can carry me most of the way. Is it far?"

"Very," the lemur says in a surprisingly deep voice. "Your feathery friend will need to stop and rest. There are trees that grow between the needles. That is where we feed. Most lemurs eat the leaves, but I prefer futfut fruit—so succulent and sweet!"

I'm not sure what this fruit has to do with us, but I

don't want to seem rude, so I wait for the lemur to open its eyes and stop dreaming about its favorite food.

"My friend needs a way to travel. He has . . . special skills, but he can't fly."

"Few can," the lemur responds. "We lemurs leap. I can carry your friend on my back."

"Really?" Vik exclaims. "That would be awesome."

Shifaka coughs into one hand and tugs at their long tail with the other. "I'm happy to help so long as you don't mind my, er, occasional indigestion." The lemur burps and looks rather embarrassed.

"No one belches louder than my little sister," Vik assures them.

"How long do you think it will take to cross the forest?" I ask.

Shifaka casts a thoughtful glance over their shoulder. "I haven't made the journey in a single day, but I'm sure it can be done. I generally travel in stages, stopping regularly to rest—and eat. The troop is much slower . . . another reason I prefer to keep my own company."

"The other lemurs seem rather standoffish."

"I didn't know lemurs could be snobs," Vik adds.

"The truth is, they object to my . . . uh . . . diet. My bad habits, really. You see, I have a particular condition that makes me . . . well . . . less pleasant to be around."

"What kind of condition?"

"It's rather embarrassing. Futfut fruit is quite delicious but doesn't always agree with me. I probably shouldn't eat so much of it, of course, but it's hard to resist and difficult to harvest. And I don't really mind being alone most of the time."

The lemur hiccups again. Then they look down at the ground and mumble, "Do excuse me."

Vik and I struggle mightily to keep a straight face as the foulest fart silently envelops us in a stink so bad it almost makes us gag.

"Don't worry about it," Vik finally manages to tell the embarrassed lemur. "We really appreciate your help."

"It's settled, then. Let's be on our way!"

Shifaka climbs down so that Vik can pull himself onto the lemur's back. We exchange silent glances as the phoenix descends as well and grabs hold of my shoulders. Then I rise above the dangerous stone daggers, and Vik lets out a joyous whoop as the lemur uses their powerful limbs to leap from shard to shard. If Shifaka has let loose another noxious fart, at least I don't have the misfortune of smelling it. The agile lemur is moving so swiftly that Vik's hair blows back. Maybe the breeze helps disperse the stench.

We make good progress, but before long, Shifaka

spots a lone tree and decides to make a pit stop. Since I'm following their lead, the phoenix and I have no choice but to pause as well. We wait while the hungry lemur reaches into the highest branches of the tree to pluck fistfuls of their favorite fruit. Only when the lemur is satisfied do they leap back to the stone needles and continue our trek across the forest.

Just when I think I can see an end up ahead, Vik makes a sound that causes me to turn back. Vik plugs his nose, which probably means Shifaka let one loose. Then the gassy lemur spies a cluster of trees that are so short they look more like shrubs. Without warning Vik, Shifaka makes a sudden dive in search of more fut-fut fruit. There's nowhere for the phoenix to perch, so we hover above the tips of the stone shards. It's a tight squeeze for the giant lemur, and the smile soon vanishes from Vik's face as Shifaka maneuvers into a deep crevice to satisfy their craving. I watch from above as the lemur makes a dramatic downward leap. Then I lose sight of the pair. All that's visible from above is the rustling of leaves.

"Vik, are you okay?" When he doesn't reply, I call again. "Vik, what's happening?"

Then I hear a terrible cry, and I know that something's wrong. Sensing my alarm, the phoenix carefully lowers me into the crevice. "Vik, where are you?"

I hear a groan, and then Shifaka appears, mouth smeared with white jelly. "Where's my friend?" I ask.

"He appears to be reclining below."

"Reclining?" With these razor-sharp rocks, there's no way Vik can be comfortable. "Can you reach him?"

Shifaka licks the last bit of juice off their fingertips and says, "I'll try."

The lemur disappears from view once more but returns a moment later. "I offered my tail, but he wouldn't grab hold. I think your friend prefers to stay behind."

"No, he doesn't!" I yell, trying to make the lemur understand the seriousness of the situation. "We have to help him. Vik, can you hear me?"

"I'm stuck!" he cries.

"Between the rocks?" I ask, wondering how I'll ever get close enough to pry him loose.

"No—I fell onto some type of web. I'm okay, Jax."

I sigh with relief and try to figure out what to do. The phoenix can't hover here indefinitely. I don't have a rope to lower to Vik, and I can't touch the stone shards that have penned him in. I think back to the Imfezi and wonder if I can use my new phoenix powers once more.

"Hold on, Vik—I'm coming!"

The phoenix carefully hovers above the spiky rocks before slowly descending. Soon I'm able to see Vik. He's sprawled on a sticky web that is layered enough to look white. I gaze up at the phoenix and try to silently communicate my plan. It seems to work; the bird gradually loosens its hold on my shoulders. I press my eyes shut and feel the warmth growing at my core. I pretend that I am making a snowball, compacting all my fear and anxiety and hope for Vik into a solid sphere of energy. When the phoenix releases me, I float in between the stone daggers. The force I am generating fills the crevice with light, and the bladelike rocks are blunted, buffed smooth.

I focus on Vik and draw closer and closer. . . .

"Don't, Jax—go away. Go away!"

At first, Vik's words don't register. I hear them but disregard them. I'm going to save my friend! "Hang on—I'm almost there." I open my eyes and reach for him. "Give me your hand, Vik."

"GO AWAY, JAX!" he hollers at me. "The light is too bright. You're hurting them. Just leave!"

Them? It takes a moment for me to realize that Vik isn't alone. At first, all I can see is the skittish vibration of the web. But then I peer closer and see the hairy tips

of long black legs. Several spiders are cowering in the shadows, forced back by the intensity of the phoenix's light. Then I realize that Vik isn't grateful or relieved to see me—he's angry.

"I can't just leave you here," I insist.

"You have to," Vik replies. "It's okay, Jax. They claimed me, remember? That's what L. Roy said. I think . . . I think they've been waiting for me to come to this place.

I think I'm meant to be here, Jax. So go find your grandfather. He needs your help. I don't."

Those last words sting a bit, but I can't make Vik accept my help if he doesn't want it. I think back to what Vonn told me that day in Chicago when we saw three bullies bothering Itzel and her grandmother. Don't swoop in and do what *you* want to do; be a waiter and find out what the other person wants or needs. Vik has given me his order, and it doesn't include me saving him from these giant spiders.

I shift myself upward and feel the phoenix's talons grab hold of me once more. As it carefully lifts us out of the crevice, I feel a pang in my heart. We take the light with us, and the last thing I see is Vik lying back upon his web bed, clearly relieved to be left alone in the dark.

"Take care of yourself, Vik," I call as my friend disappears from view.

The phoenix flies for a long while, but we don't appear to be making any progress. The forest seems neverending. I can't fly yet, but I try to generate my own energy to ease the burden of carrying me such a long distance. Finally, after what feels like hours, the stone spires begin to thin, and we reach the forest's edge. The phoenix sets me down on a rocky plateau. I sink onto a wide stone slab and feel the energy draining out of me.

"I think I need a nap," I tell the phoenix. It nods and returns to the sky. Hopefully, my own stamina will improve as I learn to manage my new powers. I take off my backpack and use it as a pillow. This evening, I'm too tired to gather wood for a fire but am warmed by a hot gust of dry air that blows up from the canyon. I can hardly bear to think about the next stage of my journey. I'll have to forge ahead on my own—because my best friend, for the first time ever, didn't choose me. Tears well up in my eyes, but I press them shut and curl my body against the wind.

"What if this is just a dream?" I whisper to myself. There is no one to respond, but I already know the answer. When I wake up, nothing will have changed. All of this is real. I am far from home. I can't call my mother because she's in Brooklyn, and I can't ask Ma for advice because she's in Chicago. I am alone here in Palmara now that Vik has chosen the spiders over me. Maybe this is how he felt when the rest of us began to share the traits of our magical friends. Right now, I would give back my phoenix powers just to have Vik by my side again. But that's not possible—even in the realm of magic, where anything seems possible. I know what I have to do. I must find my grandfather on my own.

9

The boy has no fear. Like the girl from years ago, his hair, eyes, and skin are beautifully dark. But upon our web, he does not tremble. It is as though he has been searching for us just as we have been searching for him. He is ready. Our story may begin.

The girl did not want to be claimed. She closed her ears to our plea, and her father vowed never to bring her back to our realm. This boy is different. He yearns for the chance to contribute. His elders have taught him that even the smallest creature has the power to create change.

When the light from above sears our eyes, the boy sends it away. He banishes his friend and the flaming bird, choosing the dark instead. His eyes are closed, but his mind is open. We all agree: he is the one we have been waiting for.

Without his sight to guide him, he reaches for us with his words. "Uh... I'm Vik. Do you... can you speak my language? What should I call you?"

We have many names. Ananse. Nanzi. Aunt Nancy. Hapanzi. What you call us matters little. You are here to listen. We have wisdom to impart.

The boy complies, settling himself comfortably upon our web. We knew already that his ears could hear the songs we plucked from afar. He understands he has been chosen. We have waited many years for this moment. We are ready to begin.

Strand by strand, we weave a brilliant tapestry that the boy can see without opening his eyes so that when our story ends, he will remember.

In the beginning, there was only The Dark. From the darkness came stars and planets, suns and moons. Universes expanded into infinity. Light came from The Dark, and there was balance between the two.

Here on Earth, the sea separated from the land. Far below, plates shifted, and the ground shuddered as fire from the deep spewed into the sky. Order came from the chaos, and there was balance between the two.

Life found a way forward and flourished.

All living things were bound together in a magnificent

web. Stories were woven by our kind to connect the sky, the soil, and all creatures to the people of Earth. At times, humans struggled for power, inventing tools to cause harm and spread terror. But in time, peace came from war, and there was balance between the two.

To preserve this precious yet precarious equilibrium, The Dark sent to Earth a gift. The asteroid lit up the night sky, and from that special, single egg hatched two dragons— twins. Ranabavy and Ranadahy grew quickly and came to love the world they had been sent to protect. They studied the many creatures left in their care and shifted easily between their dragon and human forms. They were feared and respected by all.

We pause to ensure that the boy's mind has not become too crowded. He is alert and engaged. We feel his mind reaching for the dangling threads of our unfinished tapestry. We spin once more and resume our tale.

Remember—before there was peace or war, before there was chaos or order, before there was light, before there was life, before there was time . . . there was The Dark. And from the darkness came the drive for balance. That urge, that impulse, that force, is known here on Earth as . . . MAGIC.

For thousands of years, the people of Earth lived with

magic in their midst. Some learned to wield it for the good of others. They studied plants and learned to harvest those that had healing properties. Only a few tried to use magic to upset the balance of life. Each time, they were foiled by the twin dragons, who could always sense the disturbance caused by greed.

The powerful siblings prevented many a plot, but over time, they realized that they could not watch over all the kingdoms of Earth. They understood that certain creatures would forever be targets of human schemes. The oldest ones possessed magic that was ancient and pure—far too great a temptation to leave within reach of those hungry for power. And so the twins gathered all the magical creatures who once lived side by side with humans. The world that had once been united was divided into two realms: yours and ours, Earth and Palmara.

Yet the separation was not complete. The two realms remained linked by a series of gates, portals that allowed select residents to travel back and forth. Gatekeepers were assigned to monitor the flow of goods and beings, but some became corrupt and could be bribed to ignore the limits set by the dragon twins. Ranabavy was vigilant and punished those gatekeepers who did not uphold the rules. But her brother was more lenient. Ranadahy was willing to turn a blind eye to the smugglers, which made *him attractive to rogues and scoundrels—and susceptible to deception.*

There was a mage from a distant kingdom who approached Ranadahy with an offer that intrigued the young dragon. King Tafar sought to bring peace to his kingdom by assembling an army that could never be defeated. Instead of the traditional weapons of war, the mage told her king, his soldiers could be strengthened by a special transfusion. All that was needed was the blood, teeth, horns, hair, and nails of Palmara's most ancient creatures. By injecting human soldiers with the essence of magical beings, the mage assured King Tafar that his army would be unstoppable. No other ruler would dare to invade their kingdom. All wars would end, and lasting peace would be achieved.

Ranadahy was intrigued. He believed the mage when she vowed no permanent harm would come to the creatures who donated their specimens. Ranadahy had always had a curious mind and less reverence for the rules his sister ruthlessly enforced. And so he agreed to sponsor the mage's experiment just to see if the transfusion would work.

The boy gasps. "It *did* work! Blue has found a way to transfer magical qualities to humans. But he didn't need to gather DNA—he used some sort of gas instead. He tried it out on me and my friends."

As we said before, unsavory types have always been drawn to Ranadahy. The mage was not satisfied with the limited specimens that the young dragon provided, and demanded that more be gathered. Smugglers rushed to satisfy her greed. This raised suspicion, and Ranabavy soon discovered their plot. She showed no mercy. Tafar and his mage were turned to stone, and their kingdom was razed to the ground. Ranadahy was stripped of his powers and banished to the Forgotten Tower.

But after a thousand years of captivity, he is seeking to do far more than mix traits. The change Ranadahy seeks can only be brought about by harnessing the power of an ancient foe, a force so dangerous it was sent to the farthest reaches of the most remote galaxy. It is called the Scourge, and Ranadahy has discovered a way to lure it back to our world.

"How?"

He used forbidden elements to create an unstable bridge that links our two realms. But the bridge emits a signal. It is, in a sense, calling to the Scourge, drawing it back to its place of origin. And once that force is unleashed upon our world, it will be impossible to contain. It is our brother, but it must be stopped.

"Brother?"

Yes. We belong to that first generation of beings who

inhabited the world when magic was free and wild and not yet codified or contained. The wizard has awakened an ancient force whose hunger for power exceeds even his own. Left unchecked, this beast will devour everything in its path. It cannot be permitted to reach Palmara, and it cannot cross Ol-Korrok's bridge.

"What must I do?"

Share with others the story we have just told you. The ancient ones have been forgotten, and with them were buried the truths that once guided your race. The world is in peril. Your friend pursues the truth, but he has been deceived. He needs the counsel of a true friend. You must make him understand—the bridge must be destroyed.

"I'll try," the boy says earnestly.

Effort is not all we require of you. You must succeed. If your leader will not do what must be done, then it will be up to you. Do not follow him to your doom. Destroy the bridge and save our world.

"But . . . my sister is here. My aunt and my friends, too. If the bridge is gone, how will we get back home?"

He hears the answer in our silence.

We ask much of you. But know that you were chosen for this task because you are worthy. Others turned away from their duty, but you will not fail us.

"Jaxon must have reached the Forgotten Tower by now. Can you help me find him?"

We carry the boy through our domain until we reach the edge of darkness. We appoint three of our kin to assist him. By the time he turns to say goodbye, we have already retreated into the safety of our shadows. We have fulfilled our mission. The true story has been told. We can do no more.

10

I have lost my best friend, but with the phoenix's help, I have also managed to cross the treacherous Forest of Needles. I'm not sure what I expected to find on the other side, but when I wake the next morning and see the barren canyon that stretches out before me, my heart sinks. In the center of the arid plateau is a lone baobab tree. Nothing else. I scan the valley but can't see anything even remotely resembling a tower. Tumbleweeds roll as hot gusts of wind stir up clouds of dust. I tell myself that I am not crying. It's just the dry air that's making my eyes water.

I take a deep breath and exhale slowly, knowing I have no choice but to rely on myself. I signal the phoenix, and it grabs hold of my shoulders and flies me over to the baobab. The baobab trees I saw on my first trip to Palmara looked so majestic, standing shoulder to shoulder along the road. Here there is no road, no path, no footprints to be found on the sunbaked earth. This tree looks ancient and unwell—its bark is withered, and the leafless branches at the very top look brittle.

When Ma and Trub were with me, the sky over Palmara was purple and I could practically feel the magic in the air. But here in this desert, nothing feels magical. The dying tree stands as a warning to anyone foolish enough to enter the canyon. I shudder and place my palm on the baobab's trunk. "Where are you, Trub?"

There is no one around to hear me, yet I barely dare to whisper the question in this desolate place. I feel an ache deep inside and brush away a few tears, but I also remind myself that I can't afford to despair—my grandfather needs me. And if L. Roy's map says the Forgotten Tower is here, then it's got to be around here somewhere. Could it be underground? Or maybe Sis found a way to make her brother's prison invisible!

Suddenly, I hear a scraping noise behind me. I turn around but see only tumbleweeds rolling across the dry earth, blown by the strong wind. I face the tree once more and am trying to come up with a plan when I feel a slight tug at my ankle. When I look down, two or three tumbleweeds have gathered around my feet. I kick them aside, expecting that the wind will help blow them away, but the balls of tangled brown vines cluster around me again. The scraping sound gets louder, and I realize that the tumbleweeds aren't being moved by the wind—they're moving by themselves!

"Ouch!" I yelp as one of the angry plant knots sinks its teeth—or thorns—into my calf. I shake my leg, but like a giant burr, the tumbleweed doesn't let go. Another latches on to my other leg, and one leaps for my arm. I angrily swat at the hungry creatures, my irritation growing as I recall how Vik saved us from the snapping fish in the Imfezi tunnel. Vik isn't here to help me now—I have to do everything by myself. "It's not fair!" I yell as I kick one of the tumbleweeds high into the air. It makes a sad sound when it lands a few feet away on the hard, dry earth, but I feel no sympathy for the strange plants. I am under attack—again—and have to defend myself.

Then the phoenix screeches, and when I look up, I remember that I have another option. I can stay on the ground and fend off the hostile tumbleweeds, or I can rise above the fray and join the phoenix in the sky. The phoenix flies up to the top of the baobab and perches on the highest branch. It squawks loudly and gestures with its head as if to say, "Come on up! Join me!"

I close my eyes and try to channel my fear and

frustration, my disappointment and self-doubt. I imagine myself packing those emotions into a sizzling sphere, just as I did back in the tunnel. As I shape the energy with my hands, eventually I feel my feet leave the ground. I only manage to rise halfway up the massive tree when the air around me stirs and I hear the flap of the phoenix's wings. I open my eyes and see it nod at me, encouraging me to continue. The phoenix waits for me to exhaust my own energy store before grasping me by the shoulders and lifting us the rest of the way up. As soon as its talons touch me, the burrlike weeds clinging to my legs squeal as though electrified. The rabid plants burst into flames, and their ash drifts away on the breeze.

The phoenix sets me down on a brittle branch. I barely have time to catch my breath before the bird squawks once to draw my attention to a square hole high in the baobab's trunk. Why would a tree have a perfectly square opening? It's not natural—someone has carved a door in the tree! "This *must* be the Forgotten Tower," I tell myself, finally daring to hope for the best. I carefully climb down the tree and fit myself inside the small opening.

"Hello?" I call, and hear my own voice echo. I turn on my phone's flashlight and hold the phone out to see into the baobab's dark depths. I'm surprised to find that the dead tree has no core—it's like someone has hollowed it out.

"Trub?" The sound of my desperate voice bounces off the baobab's empty shell. It's like yelling down an empty well.

When my echo grows silent, I hear a strange clicking sound. I glance down at the ground but already know that aside from the phoenix and those vicious tumbleweeds, I am alone in the deserted canyon. I lean closer to the dead tree and press my ear against the rough bark. The clicks are definitely coming from *inside* the baobab!

It takes a moment for me identify the familiar sound. It isn't the steady ticking of a clock. The irregular clicks sound like they're caused by a dial turning somewhere. Then it hits me—the clicking sounds like a combination lock! And who knows more about locks than a reformed burglar? My grandfather must be trapped inside the baobab. Yet the hollow tree is empty. Where is he?

I pound frantically on the thick trunk of the tree with my fists. "Trub! Trub, can you hear me? It's Jaxon. I'm here! I've found you."

But I haven't, really. If this really is the Forgotten Tower and my grandfather is locked inside, how will I get him out? Trub can pick just about any lock, but it sounds like he's struggling to break out of this prison, which was designed for a powerful wizard. If it held Ol-Korrok for a thousand years, how long will it take me to free Trub?

The phoenix caws again, so I slowly pivot to face it. The bird seems determined—almost like it has a plan. "What should we do now?" I ask. The golden bird flaps its wings to rise directly above the massive tree. With its emerald eyes trained on me, the phoenix begins to smolder. Its chest turns from orange to red and looks like molten lava!

The air around the bird shimmers with heat and magic. As its body temperature increases, my heart starts to pound in my chest. I don't know a whole lot about phoenixes, but I know they're supposed to live for a really long time—a few hundred years at least. This phoenix is only a week old. How can it be ready to die? Even if another bird rises from its ashes, it won't be the same. *This* is the bird I know. *This* is the last friend I have.

"Wait! What are you doing? Stop, stop!"

I stand up on the branch and wave both arms over my head. When I nearly lose my balance, I grab hold of the brittle branch and keep on shouting at the phoenix. "You're too young! It's not time!"

The bird is looking straight at me, but I can't tell if it's seeing or hearing me. I yell until my voice grows hoarse, but the phoenix seems to be in some sort of trance. "Don't leave me!" I plead through my tears.

Then I hear a soothing voice that is both foreign and familiar. It calmly says, "Fear not, friend, for we are ancient. Nothing can withstand the force of our magic."

If I had the same confidence as the phoenix, I might find its words comforting. Instead, I cling to my branch and watch as the flames surrounding the phoenix slowly start to change from orange to a purple shade of blue. I hold on with both hands as the tree and the earth begin to shake. I can't tell if the phoenix is turning back time or making it pass more quickly, but suddenly everything around us starts to change. Then I notice that one of its long tail feathers is turning black. But unlike the time the baby phoenix nearly burned down Miss Ellabelle's kitchen back in Chicago, the phoenix now shows remarkable control. As the single smoldering feather burns, it turns to ash. It's hard to focus on anything other than the radiant phoenix, but I pull my gaze away and look down at the ground below.

In awe, I watch as falling ash from the phoenix's burning feather transforms the entire canyon. The white ash Blue concocted sent people to sleep, but the phoenix's ash does the opposite—it revives the scorched landscape! Soft black flakes gently drift over the dry, cracked earth below, and I gaze in wonder as grass, shrubs, and even flowers begin to grow. The tumbleweeds stop rolling and put down roots in the moist soil. At the far end of the canyon, a waterfall appears, its thunderous flow feeding a wide river that winds through stands of tall palm trees. Soon the desert has entirely disappeared, and a lush valley has taken its place. Soothed by the sight of life thriving once more, I sigh and feel my racing heart begin to slow.

The phoenix, however, isn't done. Now that the valley has been transformed, the baobab itself begins to change. I hang on tight as the phoenix's powerful magic undoes the illusion Ol-Korrok must have put in place. The giant tree shudders, and strips of bark flake away. The branches all around me snap off, and soon there is only a single column of tightly stacked gray stones. Instead of sitting in the square doorway at the top of the tree, I am now sitting on the ledge of a window high in the Tower.

"You did it!" I cry, overjoyed. The phoenix nods at me and slowly lowers itself onto the ledge. The flames surrounding the bird are gradually absorbed by its body, and once again its breast looks like satiny feathers

instead of lava. I have so many questions, but I'm not sure how to speak to the powerful bird.

"Can you understand me?" I ask.

The phoenix merely nods, but its emerald eyes seem full of understanding. I sift through the many questions in my mind and decide on the best one to begin with. "I didn't know there were different kinds of magic. I mean, your magic is more powerful than Ol-Korrok's because you're older than he is, right?"

The bird nods again. Its beak doesn't open, but I hear its voice in my head. "We were among the first to be born. Our power is closer to Source."

I like how the phoenix says *we* and *our*. I don't feel all that powerful right now, but it's clear that the bond between us is growing. Have Kavi and Kenny learned how to communicate with their magical friends? I wonder what kind of conversation Vik is having with the giant spiders right now.

My second question is kind of selfish, but I ask it anyway. "Don't phoenixes live for a really long time? Like, for hundreds and hundreds of years?" I panicked when I thought the beautiful bird was about to end its life. I definitely don't want to feel that way again.

The golden phoenix tilts its head sideways, reminding me of Jamor. I wait to hear its comforting voice in my head, but there is only silence. Just as I am about to ask my third question, the phoenix says, "We will live until it is our time to die. It has always been this way."

That's not the reassurance I was hoping for, but I try to hide my disappointment by asking about Trub. "Do you know where my grandfather is?"

"Far below. Use the flame in your heart to guide you. We will wait for you here. We must rest." Then it folds itself within its wings and tucks its head into its chest.

"Right—you rest, and I'll find Trub," I whisper as I carefully turn my body on the rocky window ledge. It's a long way down! I swing one leg over and feel for the floor, but my sneaker touches nothing but air. I turn my phone's flashlight on once more and see that the round tower has a narrow spiral staircase that hugs the wall. If I drop straight down, I should land on the steps, but there's no railing. If I miss the staircase, it looks like I will fall straight to the bottom of the Tower.

Use the flame in your heart to guide you. L. Roy's map helped me find the Forgotten Tower, but is there another map inside me? I don't know what waits for me at the bottom of the Tower, but I know my grandfather needs my help. I take a deep breath and swing my other leg over the window ledge. Then I heave myself off and plunge into the blackness.

After a short fall, I land with a thud and teeter for just a moment before steadying myself against the wall with my right hand. I raise my phone above my head, and its soft glow reveals just how narrow the steps really are. I can't see the bottom of the Tower, so I just start going down the staircase. "I'm coming, Trub," I whisper to myself, cautiously placing one foot in front of the other.

After a long while descending in the dark, the staircase ends. I peer into the shadows and circle the Tower, running my hand along the cold, damp wall. I expect to find a door of some sort, but the Tower seems to have no entrance other than the window at the very top. I kneel to examine the dirt floor. A soft squeaking draws my attention to a mouse scurrying away from the lit phone in my hand. "Where did you come from?" I ask, not expecting a reply.

I swipe at the dirt with my hand and feel something cold and hard. After brushing away more dirt, I grasp an iron ring that's attached to a plank of wood. "A trapdoor!" I exclaim. My heart beats faster, and I feel a surge of confidence. Trub must be in some sort of underground dungeon.

I grasp the iron ring with both hands and tug as hard as I can, but it doesn't budge. I kneel and brush away even more of the damp earth until the entire trapdoor is revealed. Then I stand up and close my eyes. I sway in the darkness and see in my mind's eye my grandfather's smiling face, his gold tooth glinting in the sunshine. We are sitting on a bench outside Prospect Park, back in Brooklyn. It's the day we met last spring, and Trub has bought us burgers for lunch. He's telling me about jazz and how he got his name. Moments later, he will unlock the guardhouse door and take me to Palmara for the first time.

I smile at the happy memory and open my eyes. Trub opened a door for me, and now I'm going to do the same for him. The glow that was just in the tip of my index finger spreads to both of my hands. I grab hold of the iron ring and spark the fire I now carry inside me. A flame flares wildly, but I concentrate and bring it under control. Then I pull at the ring once more, and this time, I hear the door's hinges creak loudly. I turn the flame up a bit more and tug even harder at the heavy trapdoor. It groans, but I manage to lift the door several inches off the ground.

Suddenly, the door grows lighter! I look down and see a warm glow coming from underground.

"Trub—is that you?"

My grandfather's laughter makes the fire in my heart leap.

"Thought I'd give you hand, son. One more push and I think we can do it. . . ."

With me pulling and Trub pushing, we soon manage to open the heavy door. I step back and rest my hands on my knees. Trub rests his forearms on the dirt floor so only his head and shoulders are visible. Both of us are panting from exertion, and it's a while before we speak.

Finally, Trub chuckles and asks, "Should I come up, or do you want to come down? It's not all that cozy in this cell."

There's nothing to make us comfortable at the base of the Tower, either, so I say, "Let's go downstairs."

Trub winks at me. "Step into my parlor." He sweeps his arm over the doorway in the earthen floor, and I realize that my grandfather is standing on a shimmering ladder that he must have made with magic. It doesn't look too steady, but once he climbs back down, I don't hesitate to follow him. I'm curious about the dungeon but don't even bother to look around. As soon as my feet are back on solid ground, I throw myself at Trub and wrap him in a tight embrace.

When I feel his palm cradling the back of my head, I release the tears I've been trying to hold inside. Trub

lets me just cry for a while, and I let myself enjoy a few moments more in my grandfather's arms. I like channeling my emotions into energy so I can be powerful like the phoenix, but right now it feels really good to just let it all out. Trub's shirt is practically soaked by the time I run out of tears.

He cups my face with his hand and flicks away my last tear with his thumb. "This old fool must have had you pretty worried, huh?" My throat feels kind of tight, so I just I nod. "I'm sorry I put you in this situation, Jax. I didn't think I'd need anybody's help, but I sure am glad to see you. You came all this way by yourself?"

I nod again and wipe my eyes with my sleeve. Trub hands me his handkerchief and tells me to blow my nose, too. I appreciate my grandfather letting me be messy for a while and then helping me clean myself up.

"Vik was with me at first," I tell Trub, "but he told me to go on without him." I feel a hitch in my throat and swallow hard before I continue. For some reason, it's kind of hard to say these things out loud. "I didn't know what had happened to you," I explain, "but I figured it had to be something bad. Ol-Korrok . . . he seemed cool at first, but now . . . I don't know."

"You're right to doubt that wily wizard," Trub says. Then he sighs and pulls me over to a stone bench. We sit down, and Trub tells me his story in the soft glow of the magic ladder. "'Pride goes before a fall.' You know what that means, Jax?"

I think for a moment. I'm too tired to solve a riddle, but something inside me feels like I already know the answer. "Sometimes we think we're better, or stronger, or smarter than we really are?" I guess.

Trub puts his hand on my shoulder and gives it a squeeze. For just a second, I remember Ol-Korrok doing the exact same thing while we strolled along the enchanted bridge. I block the wizard out and focus on my grandfather instead. I know I can trust Trub to tell me the truth.

"That's exactly right, Jax. I must've thought an awful lot of myself to believe that someone like me could bargain with such a powerful wizard. Ranadahy offered me a deal, and I took it—but it was a trap, of course. He pulled the wool over my eyes in just a few minutes. Then he went free, and I took his place in this dungeon."

I finally take a moment to survey the dank cell. Aside from the hard stone bench we're sitting on, there's a wooden table, a wobbly three-legged stool, and a chamber pot. I wonder if it magically empties itself. Then I realize there's no way for food to be delivered. How could anyone live down here?

I don't want my grandfather to beat himself up, so I squeeze his knee and say, "It's not your fault, Trub. Ol-Korrok can be awfully convincing when he wants to be."

"Hunh—he's cunning, all right," Trub replies.

"What kind of deal did he offer you?" I ask.

My grandfather opens his mouth to speak but then changes his mind. He pulls a small volume out of his jacket's inside pocket and gazes at it with a mixture of awe and fear. Then he says, "This is a *very* special book."

I realize that must be the one book Sis allowed her brother to take to the Forgotten Tower. "He doesn't need it," I tell my grandfather as gently as I can. "Ol-Korrok told me he read that book so many times that he knows it by heart now."

Trub looks disappointed. He strokes the leather cover of the chunky book and says, "I'm not sure some-one with a heart like his can read this book—not the whole story, anyway."

"Whole story—what do you mean?" I ask. "Are some pages missing?"

Trub shakes his head and opens the thick little book. "Ever heard of a palimpsest, Jax?" When I shake my head, Trub points to the words on the page. "Look closely and tell me what you see."

I examine the page but don't see anything remarkable, so I just shrug. "It's writing—calligraphy, I guess." The book looks really old and it smells kind of musty, so the ink definitely didn't come from a ballpoint pen. Someone must have written all those words with a quill. I admire the neat lines of text and add, "Whoever wrote this book had really good penmanship."

"True—but what they didn't have . . . was paper." Trub lifts a single page and holds the book up so that the light from the glowing ladder passes through the yellowed paper. "See that? There's writing underneath the writing. Scholars used to do that when they ran out of paper. They'd take an old book that no one read anymore and scrub the ink off as best they could. Then they'd write on the bleached paper, but the old words didn't always disappear entirely. That's a palimpsest. A story written on top of another story."

All of that makes sense to me. But I'm not sure how the palimpsest proves that Ol-Korrok is especially clever. "So . . . are you saying Ol-Korrok read the wrong book?"

Trub gives me a sideways nod. "He definitely read the newer book, which does contain some powerful spells. He was able to make himself quite comfortable here, and he created the illusion that the Tower was actually a tree. But the older book—the writing underneath—is actually a lot more important because those spells are ancient. Maybe that book didn't reveal itself to Ol-Korrok, or maybe he just didn't think the older words mattered," Trub says hopefully. Then his eyes darken and he sighs heavily. "But my heart tells me that's wishful thinking. The wizard requested this particular book for a reason. He needed a key and knew he'd find it in these pages."

Keys open doors or gates. I want to ask my grandfather why Ol-Korrok needs a key when he's got a bridge, but I'm still not sure I understand why the palimpsest matters. "You said old books were scrubbed away because they weren't important."

"Most of the time, yes. But there was one book that had to be wiped because it was just too powerful—and too dangerous in the wrong hands. It's hard to know for sure, but I suspect that whoever was ordered to erase the ancient text back in the day didn't want that knowledge to be lost forever. So they wrote another book with the intention of preserving rather than destroying the most potent spells."

I consider my grandfather's theory for a moment. "So . . . whoever that person was, they must have *wanted* the two books to be read together."

"Exactly. I've only managed to make out a few of the

original lines here and there, but if we get this book to L. Roy or Sis, I'm sure they'll be able to read it right."

Trub sees me frown. He puts the book back in his jacket pocket and folds his long fingers together. "I guess Sis isn't too happy with me right now."

I nod reluctantly because it's true but it's not fair. "She thinks you deliberately helped her brother escape."

Trub doesn't look surprised. "And I bet she thinks I didn't come home because I was ashamed—or afraid to face her wrath."

"Basically," I say quietly. "What are you going to do?"

Trub gets to his feet, so I do, too. "Same thing I did when you found me: Tell the truth. Apologize. And make amends."

"Do you think the book is really that important?" I'm not so sure that a musty old book will make Sis change her mind. She believes Trub is a traitor. It might be safer to just stay out of her way.

Trub seems to read my mind, because he puts his thumb under my chin and tilts my head until our eyes meet. "Always take responsibility for your mistakes, Jax. It's humbling to admit you messed up, but you can't run away from a problem you created. Better to tell the truth, ask for help, and work to find a solution."

"Is it a problem that Ol-Korrok isn't imprisoned anymore? I mean, is he dangerous?"

My grandfather takes a deep breath. After several moments of silence, I start to think maybe Trub doesn't know the answer to my question. Then I look in his eyes and see that he's struggling to find words for something that's hard to describe. Finally, he takes another deep breath and tells me, "Prison changes a person, Jax—and not always for the better. Sis wanted to punish her brother, but she also wanted to keep the creatures in Palmara safe."

"That's why she closed all the gates," I say.

Trub nods. "Problem is, Sis didn't give Ranadahy much to do. He was a clever young man, and she made him spend century after century in this miserable tower with no one to talk to, no work, no entertainment. I told you when we first met that I got on the wrong side of the law when I was a young man." I nod, and Trub goes on. "Well, prison didn't suit me. I could feel my soul being destroyed by those bars, and the rules just didn't make any sense sometimes. Long story short, I spent some time in solitary confinement—we used to call it 'the hole.' Brothers would get thrown in there for weeks, months, even years. And when they finally came out, they were barely human."

Trub runs his hand over his face as if wiping away the memory. But I can still see the pain in his eyes when he continues. "I wouldn't wish that on my worst enemy, Jax. Being alone with nothing but your thoughts—that can break a man."

"Ol-Korrok had his book," I remind Trub, even though I know one book couldn't keep me satisfied for one week, never mind one thousand years.

"He did. And he chose it because he hoped what was inside would offer him a way to exact revenge on his sister."

"Ol-Korrok told me he had forgiven Sis."

"Did you believe him?" Trub asks. The look on my face answers for me, but Trub doesn't judge me for being duped by the wizard. "Ol-Korrok has told himself a story for the past thousand years—a story where Sis is the villain and he's the victim. Don't feel bad if he fooled you. I suspect he's even fooled himself."

"Why did Ol-Korrok choose that particular book?"

"He wanted to defy Sis. If what she wanted was to keep the realms separate, then Ranadahy was going to make sure the world was united once more—by any means necessary."

I'm starting to understand. "That's why he made the enchanted bridge. My friends and I crossed it to get from Chicago to the realm of magic. But if Sis managed to close all the gates, couldn't she just tear down the bridge?"

"I don't think it's as simple as that. A gate is a portal—a door that leads to a different realm or another dimension. There are doors that open at different moments in time. But a door is not the same as a bridge—they're different structurally and symbolically. Now, Sis is a powerful being; there's no doubt about it. But her brother's bridge isn't technically *in* Palmara. It's not under her jurisdiction, so to speak. To destroy the bridge, Sis would have to leave the realm she has vowed to protect."

"So Ol-Korrok might be using the bridge to lure Sis away from Palmara. Do you think it's a trap?"

"Could be—or just a distraction, a way to get Sis to focus on the bridge so she doesn't pay attention to what's happening in Palmara."

"Or what's happening in our world. Blue has cast a sleeping spell over New York and Chicago!"

"Ma can probably deal with that situation. But I've got a bad feeling about that bridge, Jax. I think it's just part of Ranadahy's plan."

"What's the rest of it?" I ask, feeling a knot tightening in my gut.

"We won't know until we find someone who can read this book the way it's supposed to be read."

"Kenny might be able to read it. He's dyslexic, and he read an old engraving on the wall of the spice factory that Vik and I couldn't even see."

"That's one option, then. L. Roy's smart enough to figure it out, but I think we'd better take it straight to Sis."

Trub looks a little uneasy, and I realize I'm not the only one who finds the Guardian of Palmara intimidating. "You won't have to face her alone," I assure my grandfather. "I have an audience with Sis in three days. Wait—what day is it?" I think back on my journey and try to count the number of days that have passed. "Oh no!" I cry. "Today is the third day. How will we get back to Kumba in time?"

Trub thinks for a moment. "My captain might still be waiting for me on the coast. That's the fastest way to get back to the capital. But . . ."

"But what?"

"Well, that route is kind of dangerous."

"So is the Imfezi," I tell him. "We started out safe enough in the cobra tunnel, but then there were these piranha-type fish that tried to eat us alive! With the phoenix's help, I can fly over the Forest of Needles. But how will you get across? Vik rode piggyback on a giant lemur, but I'm sure Shifaka is long gone. Plus, he farts a lot."

Trub looks at me, amused but also clearly impressed. "Sounds like you had quite an adventure getting here!"

I shrug even though I am pretty proud of myself for overcoming so many challenges and fulfilling my mission. Now we just have to find our way back and plead our cases before Sis.

"I sure would like to see the sun again," Trub says. "Let's get out of this miserable tower, put our heads together, and figure out what to do next."

I climb up the ladder first. Trub follows behind me and pulls the glowing ladder up as if it were made of string. I watch as he rolls it into a small coil before putting it in his pocket. "This may come in handy down the road," he says. And Trub is right, because once we climb the spiral staircase up to the lone window in the Tower, Trub unfurls the ladder once more, and we make our way down to the ground.

The phoenix must have had enough time to rest. I see it circling the Tower. I wave at it, and the golden bird descends from the sky. I realize Trub hasn't met the phoenix yet, so I perform introductions.

"Thank you for helping my grandson find me," Trub says with his hand over his heart.

The bird nods solemnly at him before turning toward the distant waterfall. "We are expected," the phoenix silently communicates to me.

I follow its gaze and can hardly believe what I see. There, on the ridge next to the waterfall, is a familiar black-haired boy waving his arm above his head. It's Vik—and he's seated on the back of a giant spider!

11

We reach the stone city just in time. Thanks to the giant spiders, we haven't missed our chance to plead our case before the Guardian of Palmara. I never imagined spiders could move so fast! Since there was no saddle to sit

on and no reins to hold, all I could do was use my hands to grasp the arachnid's thick, soft hair. I squeezed the firm body between my legs and just held on as best I could as Vik's new friends scrambled through a network of tunnels that passed beneath the Forest of Needles. They skirted the Abysmal Swamp, nimbly navigated the Scorched Sands, and their eight legs gobbled up the ground so quickly that we traveled quite far in a short period of time.

Now that we have arrived, the stress of the past few days suddenly catches up with me. I slump against the hairy spider, my shoulders heavy with fatigue. But then I spot my friends in the crowd gathered at the gates,

and the joy in their faces energizes me. Others who are waiting to attend the assembly see us approaching, and I hear their expressions of awe and admiration. Then everyone begins to applaud! No one in Kumba knows who I am, and Vik is an outsider, too. Trub is probably known to some folks, but I suspect the applause is for the spiders. And they deserve it—we would never have made it this far without them. And from what Vik has told us, the Great Spiders rarely reveal themselves, so leaving the safety of their underground home is a big deal. Then there's the story they shared with Vik. If it's true—and Trub thinks it is—then these amazing arachnids have shown us how to prevent war from ravaging our world.

Vik is ahead of me and Trub, and our spiders stop, waiting for their leader to advance. The phoenix flies in a casual loop overhead, sharing the sky with another winged creature that's not quite as graceful. I look closer and realize it's Kenny!

I wave at him and laugh when he hollers, "Hey, Jax— what do you call a herd of spiders?"

It sounds like the opening line of a joke, but Kenny really wants to know. I can only shrug in response, but the Professor rushes forward to enlighten us. "The correct term is a cluster or clutter of spiders." Then he surprises us all by dipping into a deep bow before the lead spider. "It is an honor—truly," he says with reverence.

Kavi approaches next, her dragon eyes flashing with alarm. Mo moves to stand beside her, and two smaller dragons with wings bring up the rear. It's hard to believe these are the three baby dragons that once fit inside the mint tin in Ma's purse! Whatever threat the spiders appear to present, Kavi and the three dragons clearly intend to tackle it together.

"What do you call a pack of dragons?" I wonder aloud.

The Professor straightens and says, "The collective term is a thunder of dragons."

Kavi gazes up at Vik, who sits astride the massive spider as if he's been traveling this way all his life. I watch as a mix of emotions transforms his sister's face. Kavi's human eyes fill with tears, and her bottom lip trembles, though she still manages to smile. "You made it—and you're all right!" she shouts excitedly. "Look, Aunty—it's Vikram!"

Kenny points at my grandfather and exclaims, "Trub's here, too! They found him!" Then Kenny makes a surprisingly smooth landing and runs over to embrace our unusual traveling party.

The spiders straighten their front legs so that we

can slide off their backs and reach the ground. It takes a while for Kenny, Kavi, Aunty, and the Professor to take turns hugging each of us. I'm anxious about the assembly, but it feels good to be reunited with our friends.

L. Roy takes off his glasses and cleans the lenses with the hem of his dashiki. "A clutter of spiders—walking above ground in the middle of the day, bringing our friends back to us . . ." Emotion overwhelms the elderly scholar. He coughs once or twice and wipes his eyes on his sleeve before putting his glasses back on. "I never dreamed I'd see such a sight. These are strange days, I tell you."

"Strange days, indeed," Aunty says, gently rubbing L. Roy's back. Her other arm is draped across Vik's shoulders, and his arm is wrapped around Kavi.

Now that the spiders are standing still, it's easier for us humans to appreciate their true size. They are half the height of Sis when she assumes her dragon form (or about twice the size of an elephant). Kavi stands before the largest spider, her mouth hanging open with no sounds or words coming out.

Vik clears his throat to get our attention and says, "Everyone, meet my new friends. This is Nyaya, and that's Umboo and Ngano."

"It's a pleasure to make your acquaintance," Aunty says politely. "Thank you for bringing my nephew home safely. We were starting to worry."

Kavi suddenly shakes off Vik's embrace and punches her brother in the arm. "You should have told us what you were up to!"

"No hitting, please," Aunty says with a stern glance. Kavi bows her head and apologetically rubs the sore spot on her brother's arm.

"Sorry for the secrecy," Vik explains, "but if I'd told you, you probably would have wanted to come with us. And Jax didn't even invite *me*!"

"It's true," I admit. "I don't know why I ever thought I could make such a difficult journey on my own."

"I definitely would have tagged along if I'd known what you were up to!" Kenny says. "But we got a lot of work done while you were away. Yesterday we polled all the magical creatures here in Kumba. At least half of them were on your side, Jax. They agreed to back you up when you make your case before Sis."

Kenny's optimism can be contagious, but today his good news only makes me frown. "They did? Sis probably won't be too happy about that."

Kavi folds her arms across her chest and defiantly asks, "Who cares? We're not here to make her happy."

Kenny grins and adds, "Sis will have no choice but to bow to the will of her people. Democracy's great!"

I sigh and search for the words I need. How do I tell my friends that I might have been duped by Ol-Korrok? The cunning wizard might even have fooled the Supreme Council. Maybe opening the gates isn't good for the two realms after all.

"I really appreciate that you two stepped up when I wasn't around to do my job. But so much has happened over the past few days." I turn to Vik and insist, "You have to tell everyone what you told us, Vik—everything your new friends shared with you. Sis needs to know what she's up against."

The Guardian might ignore a desperate kid ambassador like me, but she wouldn't dare ignore a warning from the Great Spiders. The spiders do not appear to speak as we do. Only Vik understands their silent messages. It must be time for them to leave because Vik suddenly throws his arms around the lead spider, Nyaya, just as he embraced his family members before.

"Will I see you again?" he asks hopefully.

The spider communicates an answer that pleases Vik, and he releases his friend before brushing away a tear. L. Roy asks permission to take a few photographs for his archive, and Vik says it's fine so long as the flash is off. Then he pulls out his own phone and takes a few selfies with the three spiders. Though they're from separate realms, it's clear that Vik and the Great Spiders share a special bond. I search the sky for the phoenix, suddenly feeling a little lonely. It seems to sense my solitude, because it immediately descends and perches on my shoulder. The phoenix nuzzles its beak against my face, and the ache of losing my best friend diminishes.

A gong sounds three times, and the people still outside the stone city make their way inside. Our group does the same—except for Vik. He stands on the path, his arm raised in the air even though the departing spiders can no longer see him waving goodbye.

"You coming?" I call to Vik.

He doesn't respond right away, but just as I am about to leave without him, Vik dashes up the hill and puts his arm around my shoulders.

"Just remember to breathe, Jax. I know you're nervous, but you got this, Ambassador," Vik assures me.

"Maybe Sis shouldn't open the gates. That could leave both realms vulnerable to the ancient creature the spiders told you about."

"The Scourge? I guess you might be right. But they

also told me not to despair. So now I'm telling you the same thing. We still have time, Jax. We can do this."

We were only apart for a day, but it's clear that Vik has changed. He was anxious and irritable when we first stepped foot on the enchanted bridge, but now he is calm and confident. "We'll always be friends, right?" I ask hopefully.

Vik tips his head back and laughs out loud. "Are you serious? We'll be friends forever, Jax. Aside from Kenny and Kavi, who could I talk to? Who else would understand everything we've been through—all the amazing things we've seen and done? When I want to play it safe, you show me how to be more daring. I'll never have another friend like you, Jax."

With Vik's arm around me, I feel a bit more confident about facing Sis. We follow our friends to the Great Hall. Unlike the rest of the walls in Kumba, which are made of stone, the Great Hall's smooth walls are made of red clay. We enter through tall wooden doors and wait for the assembly to begin. From what I could see during our journey to find Trub, Palmara seems to be sparsely populated. Vik and I saw no cities or villages once we left the capital, but every magical creature in the realm must have heard about today's session, because the Great Hall is overflowing.

In one corner of the room, there is a grotto with a pool for the merfolk and other aquatic beings. The floor is packed with attendees, and the high ceiling provides more space for creatures with wings. Fairies, griffins, and other flying folk hover overhead.

After hearing the loud gong before, I expect at least a little fanfare as the assembly begins. But no heralds blow their horns to announce the Guardian's arrival. Only the creaking of the massive wooden door lets us know she has entered the hall. Sis calmly circles the massive round table until she comes to an empty seat. Though she wears only a simple tunic dress, she moves as if she is wearing a regal gown with a long train. Something in her bearing makes her seem like a queen even though she is not. The chair she sits upon is not a throne. Sis folds her hands upon the table and simply says, "Let us begin."

There are a few people with complaints about un-settled debts and that sort of thing, but within about twenty minutes, L. Roy lets me know that it is my turn to address the Guardian. Just as I stand to deliver the speech I have been rehearsing in my head since Chicago, there's a scuffle out in the hallway. We hear loud bang-ing on the door, and then it gives way and a group of rowdy creatures joins the assembly.

Sis scowls at them but does not rise. "You cannot attend today's session. As you know, the terms of your quarantine require you to remain separate from—"

"We never agreed to those terms!"

The Guardian glares at the defiant gnome. "You are putting your fellow Palmarans at risk."

"We have a right to be here." Pointing at me, she adds, "The ambassador's petition may determine our fate!"

The Professor clears his throat and raises a tentative hand. Sis acknowledges him with a nod, and L. Roy nervously declares, "Actually, there is no evidence to suggest that anyone is at risk, Guardian. In fact, the symptoms I observed before seem to disappear when the creatures from Brooklyn are permitted to freely share their experiences with others."

"They are not 'from Brooklyn,'" Sis says icily. "But if you feel confident that it is safe to proceed, that is what we shall do." L. Roy nods respectfully, and Sis turns her attention back to me.

I consider reaching for my water bottle but decide to press on despite my parched mouth. "My name is Jaxon, and I have been sent by the Supreme Council. They wish you to know, Guardian, that the laws that govern our two realms . . . apply to you, too."

Sis raises an eyebrow but otherwise does not react to my opening statement. I take a deep breath and go on. "There are creatures here in Palmara who would prefer to be in Brooklyn. You took them from their home without their consent."

"It is my duty to keep all magical creatures safe. The creatures you speak of were not living in Brooklyn. As you well know, they were reduced to tattoos by the scoundrel Blue. And he would have done the same to your young friend."

I glance over at Mo and recall that night at the emporium. My mission then was to return the baby dragon to the realm of magic. But I didn't know then what I know now.

A large gold serpent raises itself from its coiled position on the floor and says, "We have all been changed by our time in the human realm. But unlike you, Guardian, we are not alarmed or afraid—we believe our time among the humans has left us enhanced rather than afflicted.

"We are grateful for the protection you have provided, but some kinds of love can be . . . *limiting*."

The Guardian snorts. "My friends, you listened to too many pop songs while you lived among the humans.

Those ballads do nothing but teach those sickened by love to let their beloved go. But I would never abandon you—I have tried to nurse you back to health."

A tiny, winged creature—not much bigger than an ant—takes the floor. They have a strange glow, and their wings are like a monarch butterfly's. For such a tiny creature, they have a mesmerizing presence. "Tell me, Sis, when did you become the enemy of innovation?" They aren't loud, but their voice is mesmerizing. Everyone—including me—gives them their full attention. "There was a time when your curiosity could not be contained."

The Professor tugs at my sleeve, and I bend down to hear what he has to say. "Yula is an aziza," L. Roy whispers. "Their kind has been known to help humans, so they may be sympathetic to your cause. Yula has also known Sis longer than anyone—except for Ranadahy, of course."

The aziza hovers above the center of the round table, their gaze locked on Sis. "When we were young, your mind reached for every opportunity to grow." Yula slowly rotates to address everyone else in attendance. "It might surprise some of you to know that Sis used to travel far and wide and read every book she came across. Only one creature had more curiosity."

"Who's that?" Kavi asks.

"Ranadahy, of course!"

Sis snarls and slaps the table with her open palm. "Do not say that traitor's name in this hall!"

Yula points their tiny finger right at the Guardian and says, "Perhaps if you had not shunned him for so long, Ranadahy might have been redeemed. Instead, he has only grown even more powerful. While you wasted time closing gates, he has built an extraordinary bridge to connect the realms you seek to divide."

Sis dismisses Yula with a wave of her hand. "We are not here to discuss my brother."

I glance at Vik, but he doesn't look as anxious as I feel. How will we explain the war that's coming if Sis refuses to listen to anyone who even mentions her brother? I decide to tell the Guardian about our new skills. "Learning to use these powers responsibly has only brought us closer to our magical friends—and proves that humans and Palmarans can work together when given a chance."

Sis just sneers at me. "It is hypocritical for you to accuse *me* of taking the creatures from Brooklyn without their consent when *you* took your friends' abilities without their permission."

"We didn't take anything!" I cry. "We never would

have absorbed their special powers if Blue hadn't exposed us to the gas he developed at the emporium."

Sis gives a scornful snort. "And yet now you are like a puppet dancing to his tune. The gifts you stole are what make these creatures precious to me."

While I am searching for a response, another brave voice speaks up. From the grotto a silver-skinned merman insists, "We are more than our gifts."

A unicorn across the room neighs in agreement before declaring, "A magical life means little if our magic cannot be shared with others."

Sis crosses her arms and says, "What if you are diminished by moving to their world? Are you really so eager to surrender your powers?"

A centaur loudly replies, "We want to know what's possible, but being under your control makes that impossible."

Sis frowns. "I have no desire to control you. If I could guarantee your safety in their realm, I would gladly open the gates and permit you to choose for yourselves. But I cannot keep you safe in that world. If you choose to live there, you must do so without my protection. It is a decision not to be taken lightly. Confer among yourselves. I will return in one hour."

Sis leaves with the same quiet grace with which she

entered the Great Hall. As soon as the door creaks shut behind her, the creatures begin having a heated debate. It's clear that some feel they are being disloyal to Sis by rejecting her protection. But most seem to agree that the gates should be reopened so that every Palmaran can decide for themselves where they want to live. When the Guardian returns, the look on her face tells me that she knows the creatures in her care have voted against her.

"If that is what you want, so be it." After uttering those words, the Guardian walks out of the Great Hall. We all follow her and watch as she calmly reaches both hands toward the sky. She bends one knee and presses her hands into the ground. Then Sis bows her head and whispers something we can't hear. There's a jolt—the air crackles with energy for just an instant—and then everything goes still.

"Is it over?" Kavi asks. "Are the gates open?"

Sis doesn't respond. She strides past us and reenters the Great Hall with Yula buzzing about her head. Vik leans in and whispers, "That felt . . . heavy."

I nod and finally exhale. I didn't even know I'd been holding my breath. Sis's simple act felt powerful . . . and final.

The creatures disperse, but my friends and I stand in

silence, each of us considering the consequences of the dramatic assembly. I have delivered my petition, but our work here isn't done. "Should we tell Sis now about her brother's plan?"

Trub can tell I'm nervous, because he says, "Why don't I speak to the Guardian alone? I owe her an explanation for my absence."

I know my grandfather is trying to bear the brunt of Sis's anger, but I have a better idea. "Let's all go in together," I suggest. "What we've learned over the past few days is that everything is connected, so let's present the facts to Sis in a way that reveals those connections."

"As a united front!" Vik says excitedly.

"Good idea," Trub says. "Let's go."

We head back toward the Great Hall. If Mama were here, I would slip my hand inside of hers. That always makes me feel strong and safe. But Mama's not here, so I hold out my arm and let the phoenix perch on my forearm. Its radiance and warmth have almost the same comforting effect.

When we enter the Great Hall, we find Sis at the far side of the round table. She is listening intently to Yula, who is standing on the tabletop. Sis frowns when she sees us and gets up from the table, clearly resentful of the interruption. The adults in our group bow their heads respectfully as she approaches, so I do the same.

"You're late." Though she's talking to Trub, somehow Sis manages to glare at all of us.

"I beg your pardon, Guardian," Trub begins. "I was trapped in the dungeon of the Forgotten Tower. I'd be there still if my grandson hadn't arrived to free me."

Sis's dark eyes glide from Trub's face to mine. "My brother tricked you."

It's not a question, but Trub answers humbly just the same. "He did, Guardian. I should have known better than to bargain with him—"

Sis arches one eyebrow and sneers as she says, "Bargain? What did you possess that you thought my brother might desire?"

Trub hangs his head. "Only the key you gave me, Guardian."

"And what could have persuaded you to give the prisoner what he wanted most?"

Trub pulls the thick volume from his jacket pocket. "This book was part of the deal, Guardian. Do you know it?" Trub asks as he offers it to her.

Sis snatches the book from my grandfather's hand.

"Of course. It is the one book I permitted Ranadahy to take with him when he left Kumba. A collection of minor spells, I believe." Sis carelessly tosses the book onto the round table, where it lands with a loud thud. Yula flies over and opens the book, silently perusing its pages while Sis speaks with us.

"I'm afraid it's much more than that, Guardian—which is why your brother requested this particular book."

Sis frowns. "What are you saying?"

Trub takes a deep breath. Then he lifts his chin, squares his shoulders, and looks Sis straight in the eye. "There are secrets in this tome that should have remained buried forever—secrets your brother now possesses."

Sis sighs impatiently and says, "Such as?"

"I believe your brother has found a way to summon the Scourge."

Sis steps back, outraged. "That's impossible!"

"Until now, yes. But Ranadahy found a way to lure it back from the far reaches of the universe—using this book."

Sis turns to Yula for confirmation, and the tiny creature nods solemnly. They turn the book so that Sis can read the text while we all wait breathlessly. The Guardian silently reads one entire page, tracing each word with her long-nailed index finger.

Trub clears his throat and finds the courage to offer some advice. "If you hold the page up to the light, you'll see that it's a palimpsest."

"I don't need light to confirm what you have said. I know what this is. How could I have been so careless!"

Yula shakes their head and puts a sympathetic hand on Sis's finger. "He is still your brother. It can be hard to believe the worst about someone you love."

Sis makes a sound of disgust and hisses, "I despise that traitor! Contempt for him must have clouded my judgment."

"Yet it was mercy that made you grant Ranadahy his request for this book," Yula insists.

"Mercy? Ha! Weakness made me give my enemy the weapon he will use to destroy everything I have created. Everything I love."

For a moment, there is silence in the Great Hall. I clear my throat to get the Guardian's attention, and when her fiery eyes are on me, I say, "You told me I was a fool to trust your brother." Sis barely nods, and it takes all my courage to hold her gaze as I go on. "Well, I realize now that you were right. Ol-Korrok told me he had forgiven you, but . . . I think he does want revenge after all.

And it looks like he's willing to start a war just to get back at you."

"Palmara has not known war for over a thousand years," Sis says with obvious pride.

Trub should be an ambassador someday, because he knows just how to make Sis hear the bad news: lead with a compliment. "Thanks to your stewardship, there has been lasting peace in this realm. And if Ol-Korrok had remained imprisoned, Palmara would likely be free of war for another thousand years. I sincerely apologize for my role in releasing the prisoner. I'm afraid that during his many years of confinement, your brother has found a way to summon a creature that lives to destroy everything it touches."

Sis shakes her head, but the grim line of her mouth suggests she knows my grandfather is telling the truth. "The Scourge was the closest Source ever came to making a mistake. It was never compatible with the other ancient ones. With its ravenous nature, the Scourge jeopardized our world's balance, and so it was sent on an impossible quest. How could my brother have found this monster?"

Vik speaks next. "It's the bridge. The magic your brother used to build it is sending some sort of signal to the Scourge. No matter how far away it is, it cannot resist the pull of the bridge. The Great Spiders explained everything to me—the bridge must be destroyed."

"That will not stop this creature from returning to Palmara," Sis says. "And once it is here, it will sniff out every trace of magic. I must meet it before it reaches our realm."

The aziza lifts themself into the air so that they are closer to the Guardian's face. "You cannot face the Scourge alone. You are the most powerful creature in Palmara. It will seek you out. We must prepare a trap."

"No! I will not allow any of my charges near this beast. I must face the Scourge alone."

The vehemence of Sis's outburst shocks us all. Yula looks hurt and flies even closer to press their hand against the Guardian's heart. "We will not allow you to sacrifice yourself."

"It may not come to that. But if it does, the choice is mine to make. I am the Guardian of Palmara."

As scary as she can be sometimes, I have always had respect for Sis. But right now, my admiration for her is even greater. "We will do our part," I assure the Guardian. "The bridge will be destroyed—I promise."

Sis turns to me with a small, sad smile on her lips.

"I have heard those words from you before, boy. Do you remember what I said to you when you first made a promise to me?"

That was after I reached the realm of magic with only two baby dragons instead of three. Back then I vowed to find the missing dragon and make things right—and I did. "I remember," I tell Sis. "You said that a promise made in Palmara carries real weight. And I told you that it means a lot in my realm, too. I didn't let you down then, and I won't fail you now, Guardian. I promise."

Sis nods at me and then turns back to Yula. "Farewell, friend. I must prepare to wage war."

"Ranabavy, please, do not face the Scourge on your own," Yula pleads. "Restore the power you took from your twin. Let him stand beside you and redeem himself in battle!"

Yula must be a very good friend, because Sis takes a moment to swallow her indignation. When she finally speaks, her voice is calm—gentle, even. "Can't you see? That is precisely why he has set this plan in motion. Ranadahy wants me to beg him to come to my aid, but I will *never* give him back his power. He would only use it to destroy Palmara—and me."

"If you don't combine your strength, the Scourge will do the same."

Sis sighs heavily and tells Yula, "You must be true to your nature, as I must be true to mine. Offer the humans whatever assistance they require."

Yula nods and trails after Sis as she strides across the Great Hall and exits through its massive wooden doors. The glowing butterfly-like creature returns to us and in a stern voice says, "There is much to do, but first I must tell you just what is at stake if you fail."

12

I could sure use a pep talk right now, but Yula seems determined to bring the gloom and doom. We gather around the aziza as they take us back in time to the days when Sis was that young, inquisitive dragon-girl Yula mentioned during the session.

"When magic was new to the world, spells were never written down. It was not necessary, for magical knowledge was passed from one practitioner to another orally. That is still the way it's done in many communities. But as the ancient ones began to withdraw from our world, one sorcerer realized that much would be lost, and so he gathered as many spells from the elders as he could. And he wrote them in a book. It was called the Hungwaru.

"This book was considered so valuable—so sacred— that it was kept in a vault in the library here at Kumba. Sis, eager to read everything of any significance, asked permission to read the Hungwaru, and it was granted. Inside she found the spell that later enabled her to strip her brother of his power. But despite efforts to keep it hidden, word of the precious book of spells reached the ears of those craving the power that only comes from old magic. It was decided that the book would be destroyed. The spells were wiped from its pages, and a new, harmless text was printed on the blank pages.

"But ancient magic is not so easily destroyed. The pages retained the original words even after other spells were written over them. The effect was to compound the power of the original enchantments. In a sense, the book holds a powerful blend of magic, old and new. I suspect it took Ranadahy centuries to teach himself how to read both sets of spells together." Yula smiles ruefully as they remember the young dragon-boy. "Even as a child, he could be very determined once he set his sights on something he desired."

I ask, "Do you really think he would agree to fight alongside Sis if she restored his power?"

"I honestly don't know. Perhaps Sis is right— Ranadahy might turn on her. But she cannot destroy the Scourge on her own. It is drawn to power, and that makes her its primary target."

For a moment, none of us speak as we contemplate

the fact that there is no one to guard the Guardian. I wonder for the first time if Sis is lonely. Perhaps that's why she made Ma promise that she would retire and move to Palmara for good. What would happen to Palmara if the Guardian fell in battle? What would happen to the human realm?

"If Sis is defeated, will the Scourge cross into our realm?" I ask.

Yula nods gravely. "The gates have been opened. No doubt many magical creatures have already made the journey back to your world. The Scourge will track those creatures and pursue its quarry wherever the scent leads. Fortunately, the vast majority of humans don't have magical powers, so they are less likely to attract the beast."

"We do," Kavi says quietly. Mo, Lex, and Rex instinctively form a protective circle around her.

"She's right," Kenny says. "We have magical powers now. So that means the four of us are at risk."

I gasp. "And Ma—and Mrs. B., Quayesha, and Dutch. Everyone who was at the witch convention in Chicago is in danger!" Desperate for answers, I draw closer to Yula. "What exactly does the Scourge *do* to its prey?"

Yula looks first to the adults and then to us kids. I sense them deliberating. Ultimately they decide to tell us the unvarnished truth. "The Scourge feeds on magical creatures. It is like a sponge—"

"A leech, you mean."

"Yes—perhaps that is more accurate. The Scourge feeds off the special abilities of others, leaving them drained of their power. For humans such as yourselves, an encounter with the beast would merely leave you human in the most ordinary sense. But for someone like Sis . . ." Yula shudders, and their dark eyes shine with tears. "The last time the Scourge was unleashed on Palmara, we lost one of our more ancient elders, Imfezi."

"The cobra!" I cry, understanding how the giant snake came to be a fossil.

Kavi wraps an arm around Mo, and Kenny reaches for Jef, who is perched on his shoulder. "We have to do something!" he insists.

"How do we destroy the bridge?" I ask. The four adult humans say nothing and avoid my gaze, but Yula is more forthcoming.

"Ranadahy used a spell from the Hungwaru to build the enchanted bridge. Only magic more powerful than his can undo what he has done."

I remember what the phoenix told me before it reversed the spell Ol-Korrok had placed on the Forgotten Tower. "Old magic is the most potent, right?"

L. Roy and Trub exchange sly glances, which is as good as having both of them say yes. Yula nods and says, "Do you have a plan?"

"Sort of," I tell her. "I'm still learning how to use my power, but it comes from the phoenix. Maybe together— old magic and new—we could undo the enchantment Ol-Korrok cast on the bridge."

Yula's eyes open wide. "A phoenix? Where is this wondrous bird? I would like to see it before I go."

"Go?" Kavi says, looking panicked. "Can't you stay and help us?"

"We each have a role to play. I have known Ranadahy since he was no bigger than your young dragon friends." Lex and Rex must know Yula is talking about them, because they lift into the air and hover above the table. "Sis cannot face the Scourge alone, but she is too proud to ask her twin for help. I must do what she will not."

"You're going to the human realm?"

Yula nods, and Trub says, "Then take the children with you. They ought to be at home with their parents."

All four of us erupt at once. Kenny stamps his foot and cries, "No way!" Shaken from his perch, Jef pats Kenny's shoulder soothingly.

Kavi objects, too. "That's not fair," she snarls before reining in her rage. "We can help if you give us a chance!"

"Like Yula said—each of us has a role to play," I remind Trub. "I have to help the phoenix destroy the bridge. It'll protect us. Right, Vik?"

To my surprise, Vik doesn't answer right away. Instead, he puts his arm around Kavi and says, "Actually, I think we're going to stay here with Aunty."

Kavi's face lights up. "And Mo!"

"And the spiders," I mutter.

Vik steps closer and puts his hand on my shoulder. "Try to understand, Jax. You've had a job for a while—more than one, really. Now I have one, too. I'm the only one who can hear the spiders' web songs. If they send a message, I need to be here to receive it."

"And my thunder needs me," Kavi adds.

I glare at the floor, but Vik dips down to make me look him in the eye. "We're still on the same team even if we're working apart. Right?"

I lift my head up and nod at him. "Right."

Trub still looks anxious, but his voice is resigned. "In that case, Jax and I will take the phoenix to the bridge."

L. Roy coughs nervously, which suggests he disapproves of my grandfather's plan.

"What?" Trub asks rather irritably.

"Well, it might be more . . . er, *prudent* . . . if you were to be on the other side . . . just in case anything goes wr— I mean it might be best if you were waiting in Chicago to welcome Jax. Maybe Ma could join you—just in case."

Trub thinks for a moment. Then he grunts and says, "You're asking an awful lot of my grandson. He's just a kid, L. Roy."

"I can do it, Trub," I say with more confidence than I actually feel, though the thought of Ma being at the other end of the bridge makes me feel better.

Trub tries to smile at me, but I see the sadness in his eyes. "I'm not sure you understand, Jax. You would have to cross the bridge and destroy it once you reach the human realm."

"Not after—*before*." My confusion must show on my face because L. Roy takes time to explain it to me. "Theoretically, Jax, you need to deliver what amounts to a magic 'bomb' if you want to destroy the bridge."

"But I haven't got a bomb. Unless you mean . . . the phoenix?"

"Precisely! Once you've attached it to the middle of the bridge, you would need to set the timer, so to speak, and get off the bridge before the bomb detonates. That, I'm afraid, is our best option."

My stomach drops. "How can I cross the bridge and destroy it at the same time?"

"You can't," Trub growls. He's glaring at the Professor, not me, but L. Roy isn't to blame for this dilemma. I'm mostly worried about the phoenix. When it "detonates," will it die?

"You can," L. Roy insists. "But, as they say, timing is everything."

"I'll go with you," Kenny offers. "I can fly pretty fast now, so maybe I can buy you some time somehow or distract the Scourge while you blow up the bridge."

That does sound potentially helpful, and at least I won't be out there on the invisible bridge in outer space by myself. I turn to Vik to get his opinion. "What do you think?"

Vik's forehead creases like it always does when he's thinking something through. He doesn't try to hide his concern, but Vik finally says, "I think it's worth a try. I'm going to see if I can reach the spiders. Maybe they have some advice for us."

I feel a flicker of resentment, but Vik squashes it by throwing his arms around me. "Good luck, Jax," he whispers in my ear. "You can do this. And remember— we've got your back."

I hug my best friend, knowing this might be the last time I see him for a while . . . or forever. "Thanks, Vik. Take care of yourself and your family."

"I can take care of myself," Kavi insists as she follows her brother toward the exit, with the three dragons right behind her. "We're going to find Sis. She doesn't have to wage this war on her own—not when there's a thunder of young dragons in Palmara!"

It's hard to imagine Sis accepting aid from Kavi, Mo, Lex, and Rex, but I'm sure they'll find some way to contribute to our cause. Trub, L. Roy, and Aunty huddle together, so Kenny and I leave them to their private conversation. Yula flits between us, occasionally exchanging words with Jef.

"Is an aziza the same as a fairy?" I ask Kenny.

"I think they're like cousins," he tells me. "Part of the same family."

I nod and scan the sky above the stone city. "I'd better tell the phoenix what we've got planned," I say. As always, the golden bird finds me first. When it lands on my outstretched arm, the look in its eyes tells me the phoenix already knows about the weighty task that lies ahead.

"The enchanted bridge has to be destroyed. We can do it together, can't we? I'll generate as much energy as I can so you don't have to use up all of yours." The phoenix nods, but I hear the echo of its words in my mind:

We will live until it is our time to die. It has always been this way.

Yula pulls me back to the present moment by wishing us luck. "I will do my best to persuade Ranadahy to support his sister. Their feud is an old one. It's time to heal the rift between the twins and the two realms. If you succeed in destroying the bridge, the world may once again be united as it was in the beginning."

"No pressure," Kenny quips, and I almost manage to laugh.

"Do your best, young man. That is all Palmara expects of you."

As the aziza flies away, the adults exit the Great Hall. "Ready to go?" Trub asks.

Kenny and I nod. Aunty says she's going to check on her niece and nephew, but she gives both of us hugs first. "Youth has its advantages. Children see the world as it is, and yet they also see all its possibilities. Let your vision of a better world guide you, boys." Aunty turns to L. Roy and Trub. "We elders must unlearn some of the lessons we have been taught. I never imagined the fate of the world would lie in the hands of four children, but we must try to expect—and accept—the unexpected."

Aunty waves before heading down the winding alley

that leads to her compound. The rest of us walk in the opposite direction and soon pass through Kumba's tall gates. We don't say much until the grassland ends and we see the shore.

"This is where we part ways," L. Roy says. "There's a portal not far from here. I'll take your grandfather there and return in case . . . well, er, in case you should need my assistance. Even if you can't see me, know that I'll be here on the shore rooting for you."

"Thanks, L. Roy," I say before giving him a hug. He leads Kenny away so I can have a private moment with my grandfather.

"It's not too late to change your mind," Trub says.

I want to assure my grandfather that I'm not afraid, but that would mean telling a lie. So instead, I wrap my arms around his waist. Trub kisses the top of my head, and for a full minute, we don't say a word. When I finally pull myself away, Trub takes me by the shoulders and looks into my eyes. "Trust your intuition, Jax. Magic is amazing, but each of us is born with a gift in our gut. If you feel your body telling you to quit and run, then that's what you do. Okay? You don't have to be the hero."

My dad gave me the opposite advice. He always told me to try again if I messed something up the first time. *Don't be a quitter—be a striver.* My dad would have made a great coach, but he got stuck with a son who wasn't any good at sports. His advice still applies in other areas of my life, and even though Dad isn't around anymore, I still think of myself as a striver. So why is Trub giving me permission to give up?

"I'll listen to my gut," I promise my grandfather. He gives me another hug and then quickly walks off. L. Roy waves at me and hurries to catch up with Trub.

Now it's just me, Kenny, and our magical friends. We stand on the shore of the Black Sea, searching for the end of the enchanted bridge.

"I'll go first," Kenny says before lifting himself into the air. Jef zips ahead and guides him to the point where the bridge abruptly stops. Kenny makes another perfect landing and turns back to wave at me. Without being asked, the phoenix grasps my shoulders and lifts me into the starry purple sky. "I can cross over by myself," I say.

The phoenix silently responds, "Save your strength for the task to come."

The bridge bounces slightly as we walk. "Did it do that before?" Kenny asks, trying to sound simply curious and not nervous.

I hold my arms out to steady myself. The bridge is swaying, too. "Nope. Something's definitely changed."

"Maybe Ol-Korrok designed the bridge so it would self-destruct. Or self-disintegrate."

"That would be great if we knew exactly when it would disappear."

"Hopefully not while we're trying to blow it up," Kenny says. "By the way, I've been meaning to ask: How do we destroy this bridge? We don't actually have a bomb or a timer or a detonator."

"That was just a metaphor," I tell him. "The phoenix can generate enough energy to undo Ol-Korrok's spells. It did that once before, at the Forgotten Tower. With my help, we should be able to produce a fire so powerful that it undoes the enchantment."

"Cool," Kenny says. His casual tone makes me chuckle. Except for the galaxy swirling above us, we look like a couple of kids out for a stroll in Brooklyn. We could be heading to the bodega for a snack—but we're not. We're trying to save our friends and our world from a monster we've never even seen.

"I'm glad you're here, Kenny. I would've come on my own if I had to, but . . ."

"We wouldn't have these special powers if it weren't for you, Jax. So it only makes sense that we use our abilities to help you. We're a team, right?"

"Right."

"Go, Team Mutants!" Kenny cheers with his fist raised in the air. "No, wait—I can do better than that. The Magical Mutants! Or . . . the Extraordinary Experimentals. Is that even a word?"

Kenny's chatter is comforting and a welcome distraction as we cross the unstable bridge. We walk for several more minutes but stop when the phoenix screeches overhead.

"That doesn't sound good," Kenny says. "Do you speak phoenix? What does 'KRAAAAAAGH' mean?"

The phoenix hasn't spoken to me, but I understand its meaning just the same. "This is where we do it," I tell Kenny. "This is where we ignite the flames that will destroy the enchanted bridge."

Kenny takes a deep breath and asks, "Where should I stand? Here? Or farther back? I don't want to lose my eyebrows again. It happened once before, when I was six. I was playing with matches. Stupid, I know . . ."

"You and Jef keep going. We'll catch up once . . . I mean, after . . . you know."

"Okay, sure, we can do that. I'm not gonna say goodbye, because I'm gonna see you in just a few minutes, right?"

"Right," I assure him. "It probably won't take much longer than that." I don't even know what *it* is, but we both act like nothing out of the ordinary is about to happen. The phoenix screeches again, and Kenny wisely starts moving. I wave and swallow the selfish plea for my friend to stay with me a bit longer.

"See ya, Jax," Kenny says as he starts walking backward down the bridge, trying hard to smile.

I wave and then turn my back to Kenny. It's time to focus on the phoenix, since it's the only one that knows what's supposed to happen next. I have to squint as I look up at the glowing bird. The darkness all around us seems to retreat as the phoenix prepares to ignite.

"What should I do?" I ask.

"Follow the flame in your heart," the bird communicates silently.

I close my eyes against the intensifying light radiating off the phoenix and think about what's at stake. Trub said I didn't have to be a hero, but I can't stand by and watch my friends get hollowed out by the Scourge. I think of Ma, and Mo, and Sis. The Guardian isn't the only one who wants to keep the magical creatures of Palmara safe. If the phoenix and I can stop the Scourge from entering the two realms, maybe that would inspire trust in humans.

I hold my hands in front of my chest and begin shaping my emotions into a fiery ball of energy. Opening my eyes, I focus on the phoenix's gleaming green eyes. No tears fall from the bird's eyes this time, but as before, flames fan out from its body, and its chest looks like molten lava. For just a second, I worry about being scorched by the intense heat, but then I look up at the phoenix and realize that the space between us has disappeared.

I am no longer standing on the invisible bridge—my body is rising toward the flaming bird hovering overhead. When I am close enough, I take the burning ball of energy and press it into the phoenix's chest. The light we are creating no longer blinds me. With eyes wide open, I watch as the bridge beneath us begins to shatter. The cracking is audible and seems to energize the phoenix even more. I fight the urge to celebrate, and continue to follow the ancient bird's lead.

For the first time, I feel like I really am part of the phoenix. I am young and I am human, but I'm still able to feed its ancient fire with my own fuel. Beneath us, the bridge comes apart, and jagged chunks of glass spin into the void. I am trying to focus, but at the back of my mind is the hope that Kenny crossed over in time.

Suddenly, I hear a high-pitched scream coming from the depths of the starry expanse. The phoenix's emerald eyes flash with recognition—the Scourge must be near!

Next, I hear the bird's voice in my head. "Our work here is done. You must go—now!"

The phoenix begins to pull away from me, but I am not ready to break the bond between us. "Come with me," I say aloud.

Another scream tears across the normally silent galaxy. The phoenix clenches its talons and, with its feet shaped like fists, forcefully thrusts me away. "Flee, Jax—FLEE!"

Behind the phoenix, I see a white haze spreading over the darkness. The vapor doesn't look menacing, but the alarm in the phoenix's voice prompts me to obey its command. Still brimming with unspent energy, I press my own fists into my thighs and roll onto my stomach. Like a rocket, I launch myself in the direction of Cloud Gate. With the bridge destroyed, it's hard to know for certain that I'm going the right way. But my gut tells me I'm heading home, and Trub said to trust my intuition.

Sure enough, within a few seconds I see the bean-shaped fun house mirror up ahead. Kenny and Jef hover before it, clearly relieved to see me coming. "Go, go, go!" I holler.

My two winged friends hurriedly pass through the gate, but I bring myself to a halt and look back, hoping to see the phoenix. The white mist seems to be spreading in every direction, swallowing stars as it advances. It crackles as it consumes everything in its path and grows whiter and more opaque, like a glittering blanket of freshly fallen snow.

Refusing to be seduced by the Scourge, I scan the sky for my golden friend. "Please be okay, please be okay," I say over and over. Suddenly, the phoenix rears high above me in the sky, as if struck by an invisible fist, and lets out a screech that raises every hair on my head. I see a trail of shimmering purple stardust leading from the phoenix, and when I follow it back to its source, I see a giant dragon hovering in space. It's Sis! She says something in dragon-tongue, but I can't tell if she's talking to me, the phoenix, or the Scourge, because the white mist has almost enveloped all three of us. Then Sis hurls herself into the vapor, and I hear another terrifying scream.

The phoenix races toward me, grasping my knapsack with its talons. It knocks me through the gate, creating an explosive spray of bright orange sparks, and then the golden bird disappears.

13

I fall out of the giant silver bean and land with a painful thud on the pavement below. Kenny is there to lend me a hand, and when I'm back on my feet, he asks, "What happened back there?"

I'm not sure, so I just shrug. "Have you seen the phoenix?"

Kenny shakes his head and turns to Jef, who makes the same gesture. "Only you passed through the gate," he tells me. "Maybe the phoenix turned back after dropping you off?"

"Maybe," I say, searching desperately for another possibility. "Sis was back there—and so was the Scourge. It looked like they were about to fight."

"Whoa," Kenny says, pulling his fairy friend close. "Don't worry—I'm sure Sis will win," Kenny assures Jef. The fairy doesn't look as certain—and neither do I.

"Where's Trub?" I ask. "My grandfather was supposed to be here waiting for us."

"Maybe he used a different gate," Kenny suggests. "Trub's probably around here somewhere." I must look worried, because Kenny tries to lift my spirits by stating, "At least you destroyed the bridge."

"Yeah, we did," I reply. It's a big deal, yet I feel anything but triumphant right now. I remind myself that the phoenix has left me before, but it always returns when I need it. And I don't need the phoenix right now, because our mission has been accomplished.

Kenny puts his arm around my shoulders and gives me an encouraging squeeze. "Congratulations, Jax—you saved the world! Um . . . are you okay?"

I open my mouth, but for some reason, no words come out. My stomach feels a bit queasy, and my chest aches from being punched by the phoenix's balled feet. We destroyed the enchanted bridge and prevented the Scourge from entering our world. That's exactly what the Great Spiders told us to do. So why do I feel so uneasy? And why did the phoenix flee?

I don't want to talk about myself right now, so I change the subject. "Think Vik and Kavi will be okay in Palmara?"

Kenny nods. "Sure. They've got L. Roy and their aunt

to look out for them—plus the spiders and Mo. Our friends will find a way back to our world once it's safe," he assures me.

I know I should take the lead and come up with a plan, but I feel like I am frozen. My strange state worries Kenny, who finally says, "Well, guess we better get back to Brooklyn."

I manage a nod, and we leave the shelter of the over-sized bean. Millennium Park looks like a winter wonder-land. I hold out my hand to catch some snowflakes, and my suspicions are confirmed—it's ash. Blue must have accelerated his plan to sedate all the adults in the city. As we walk through the empty park, I wonder if New York has been blanketed, too. Will Mama even be awake when I get back to Brooklyn?

Kenny, Jef, and I trudge up Michigan Avenue and make our way to the UR station. The bronze lions stand guard outside the Art Institute, totally indifferent to us now. The five Great Lakes statues are frozen above the dry fountain, unable to hold our hands and guide us along.

"Think Dutch will be waiting for us?" Kenny asks as we jointly push against the heavy stone door that leads underground.

"I don't know," I reply. "I sure hope so. I don't know how to drive the UR!"

We descend the steep stairs, drawn by a dim light below. When we reach the platform, my heart leaps—it's Trub! He's holding a lantern, but he hangs it from a hook on the wall and tells us to hurry. "Hop on board!"

We slip inside the glistening vehicle and buckle up. Trub looks confident as our conductor, and he winks at me over his shoulder. "Sorry I couldn't meet you at the gate. The convention is over, but the Supreme Council called everyone back for an emergency meeting. That scoundrel Blue has got Ma and her team working overtime, so I told Dutch I'd cover for her down here."

"Have you driven the UR before?" I ask.

"Once or twice," Trub says nonchalantly. "Ready?" Kenny and I nod, and Jef finds a secure place to sit in Kenny's vest pocket. The UR lurches forward, then backward. Trub apologizes and pulls on the gear, sending us speeding through the darkness. My stomach is still churning, so I'm glad it won't take long for us to leave Chicago behind and get back to our families. I think Kenny's worried about what to tell his mother. I'd like to help him out, but I have my own problem to solve. I need to talk to my mother. If the spiders are right, all this drama could have been prevented if she had helped them thirty years ago. I need Mama to tell me everything. I need to know how she set in motion the chain of events that unleashed the Scourge.

Trub parks the UR in the Prospect Park station and presses the hidden switch on the rock wall that lowers the paving-stone staircase. We walk silently through the park, made wintry by steadily falling ash, and soon reach the exit on Flatbush Avenue. Trub steps away to take a phone call, leaving me and Kenny alone for a moment.

"I've decided to tell my mom the truth," Kenny confides. "It's too much work coming up with excuses and stories every time something magical happens. Plus, I want her to meet Jef."

I think Kenny's brave to come clean like that. "What do you think your mom's going to say about your new abilities?" I ask.

Kenny shrugs and says, "There's only one way to find out!"

We hug, and then Kenny heads down the block with Jef tucked safely in his pocket. Not that there's anyone out on the street to notice the fairy. Brooklyn is eerily quiet instead of loud and bustling, like it should be. Trub comes over to where I'm standing. "Everything okay?" I ask.

Trub shivers and blows on his hands before saying, "Not yet, Jax, but this is just the beginning. A wise woman once told me, 'Everything will be okay in the end. If it's not okay, it's not the end.'" Trub winks at me and pulls up the collar of his coat. "For now, let's get outta this ash. Ma gave me a dose of silver root back in Chi-Town, but I don't want to take any chances."

We huddle together and hurry up the block toward

Ma's building. There are things I want to say to Trub that I didn't feel comfortable talking about in front of Kenny. Now seems like a good time to talk. "You haven't asked about the phoenix," I say quietly. "Did something bad happen to it?"

Trub frowns. "I don't know, son. But a phoenix has more lives than a cat, so don't you worry about that beautiful bird. It knows how to take care of itself."

I know the phoenix is basically immortal, but I doubt that the next bird to be born will be the same as the bird I've come to know and love. I think about Trub's advice and check to see what my gut is telling me. My stomach lets out a loud growl, making my grandfather smile.

"Maybe we'd better pick up a couple of burgers on the way home," he suggests. I agree, and a few minutes later, we let ourselves into Ma's apartment carrying grease-stained paper bags. Trub has already devoured half of his cheeseburger, and I am ready to inhale mine! The smell of french fries makes my mouth water, but I only have time to shove three into my mouth before Mama storms into the kitchen.

"Where have you been, Jaxon? I've been looking everywhere for you!"

I swallow hard and glance at Trub, hoping he's got my back. My grandfather sheepishly takes another giant bite of his burger, leaving me to answer the question myself. I think about Kenny's plan to tell his mother the truth and decide to do the same.

I'm sorry, Mama. I had to save the world from an ancient, ravenous beast called the Scourge. I try that line out in my head and decide I'd better take a different approach. "I'm sorry, Mama. I should have told you where I was going, but . . . well, I thought you might try to stop me from going to Palmara to look for Trub."

Mama just stares at me for a moment. Then she pulls out her phone and reads aloud the text I sent her. "'Hi, Mama. Going on a mission with Trub. Ma will explain. Be back soon.'"

"'I love you.'" Whenever I say that, Mama usually says, *I love you, too, baby,* but right now she just scowls at me.

"Don't try to sweet-talk me, young man."

I hear familiar scratching at the window but can't afford to let myself get distracted right now. "I wouldn't do that, Mama," I insist. "That's how I ended my text— 'I love you'—but you left that part out."

Now that his burger is gone, Trub brushes the crumbs off his beard and says, "Don't be too hard on the boy, Alicia. The truth is, Jax went to Palmara to rescue me. I was in a tight spot and—"

Mama rolls her eyes. "*Of course* you were. Daddy, you promised me you wouldn't get my child into trouble. But that *is* your name, so what did I expect?"

"Don't be mad, Mama," I plead. "I did something really important! With the phoenix's help, I destroyed the enchanted bridge. The wizard Ol-Korrok built it so he could send a signal to lure the Scourge back to Earth—"

"STOP!" Mama yells. Then she takes a deep breath to calm herself. "Just stop, Jax," she says in a gentler tone. "*This* is why I didn't want you mixed up with magic. You're not even making sense right now, but I know you put yourself in danger. Didn't you?"

"The world is full of danger, Alicia. You can't lock the boy up just to keep him safe," Trub says.

"I don't need *you* to lecture *me* about parenting," Mama snaps.

I appreciate my grandfather's help, but I hate to see Mama directing her anger at Trub. He wasn't around much when Mama was growing up, but Trub has apologized and right now he doesn't make any excuses or even try to defend himself. Instead, he says, "Fair enough—I'm certainly no expert on that particular topic. But I do know a thing or two about magic. And your son has a gift, Alicia."

"A phoenix this time, is it? Did you trade in the three dragons from before? Just like Jack and the Beanstalk!" Mama adds sarcastically.

Now it's my turn to scowl. I know I've let Mama down, but that doesn't give her the right to mock me or my magical friends. "No," I say as tersely as I dare. "Vik gave me a phoenix egg before I left for Chicago, and when it hatched, I took care of it. The dragons are in Palmara with Kavi. Vik has been claimed by the spiders, and Kenny's at home right now trying to explain to his mother why he can fly like a fairy. We all share the special powers of the magical creatures we met." My mother's eyebrows are higher than they've ever been before. She looks more amazed than angry so I add, "There's a lot I wanted to tell you, Mama, but . . . you make it hard sometimes."

Mama sighs and sinks into one of the chairs at the kitchen table. She reaches for some of my fries and munches on them silently for a while. I use this opportunity to take a bite of my burger. The squirrel raps on the glass with her tiny fists, and I shake my head to signal that now's not a good time to visit.

Mama licks a couple grains of salt off her lips and says, "I want you to tell me the truth, Jax, because it's my job to take care of you. And I can't do that if you're not honest with me."

"You haven't been entirely honest with me, either, Mama." I try to state it delicately so it sounds like a simple fact and not an accusation. But I still see anger flare in Mama's brown eyes.

"What are you talking about?" she demands.

"I need you to tell me about the time Trub took you to Palmara." I see Mama shudder before she looks away. "I know you didn't like it there . . . but I need you to tell me why. It's important, Mama. Really important."

Mama closes her eyes for a moment and sighs heavily. "That was a long time ago, Jax. I had nightmares for months afterward. I've tried hard to erase that terrible journey from my memory."

"Because of the spiders?" I ask.

Mama's mouth falls open, and fear flashes in her eyes. "H-how do you know about them?" Mama grips my arms and fearfully asks, "Did they get you, too? Did they hurt you?"

I quickly shake my head and try to reassure my mother. "The spiders only appear to certain people, Mama. They claimed Vik, not me, because I'm not marked. But I think you are—or were."

"Marked? Don't be ridiculous, Jax. I'm sure those big, nasty bugs trap anyone foolish enough to wander into their disgusting web. I was just a child then. I didn't know where I was going or what I was doing. Everything was new and strange and unfamiliar. . . ."

For a moment, Mama drifts away. She's still sitting in front of me, but I can tell by the look on her face that she's reliving whatever happened thirty years ago. When I take her hand in mine, she jumps. "I know it's hard, Mama. But I need you to tell me everything that happened to you that day."

Mama props her elbows on the kitchen table and rests her head in her hands. The squirrel tries once more to get my attention, so I toss a balled-up napkin at the window. She finally takes the hint and leaves us alone.

"I thought Daddy was right behind me," Mama recalls, "but I guess I had wandered farther than I realized. There was this . . . music. It was so unusual, and I wanted to find its source, so I ventured into the woods. At first, I just felt wisps of silk brushing against my skin. That didn't alarm me—it kind of tickled. But then the forest got denser and darker . . . the music got louder, and I wanted to turn back but I couldn't. It was as though something had hooked me like a fish, and it was just reeling me in. I didn't know how to resist the pull . . . and . . . I didn't want to. I didn't feel like myself at all."

"The music you heard was the spiders' web songs," I explain. "Vik hears it, too, but the rest of us can't."

"I hope I never hear it again for as long as I live!" Mama declares. "It was beautiful in an eerie sort of way, but when the music stopped—they were there. Dozens of hairy, disgusting spiders—they came in every size from tiny to gigantic. It was like facing an arachnid army! Whatever trance I'd been under ended abruptly, and I screamed. What else could I do? I was terrified. I turned to run, but they had made a web behind me. I ran straight into it, and I was stuck—I couldn't move. Then a wad of that awful sticky substance was in my mouth, choking me. . . . I guess they were trying to keep me quiet."

Mama pauses and looks at Trub. "Your grandfather heard my cries. He came through the woods slashing at everything with some type of glowing blade. . . . He was my hero that day. He promised me we'd never come back and that he'd never let anything bad happen to me ever again." Mama manages a weak laugh. "I guess he kept one of those promises, at least. I never set foot in Palmara again—and I never will. And neither will you, Jax. This family is DONE with magic!"

Mama fastens her eyes on my face so I know she's serious. I want to tell Mama she's wrong. She can make that decision for herself if she wants, but my mother can't choose a magic-less future for me and Trub. I can't deny I've made a few mistakes since becoming Ma's apprentice, and sometimes it's hard for me to know who can be trusted and who can't. But I'm proud of the person I've become. I wish Mama was, too.

The squirrel returns and frantically bangs on the window with open palms. We all turn to look, so we don't see who's standing in the doorway. I jump when I hear Ma's gruff voice behind me. "You really gonna leave your little friend out in the cold this time?"

"Ma!" I jump up and rush over to give her a hug. She hands me a shopping bag and shuffles over to the kitchen table. Ma's still wearing her puffy purple winter coat, and it makes a sad deflating sound as she takes a seat across from Mama at the table. Stuffing a handful of fries into her mouth, Ma nods at the bag and says, "Bring me a beer, boy."

I do as I'm told, pulling a six-pack of root beer from the bag and setting it on the table. I twist the caps off four bottles and give one to everyone, starting with Ma. She takes a sip before opening the window and letting

224

the squirrel inside. She chatters loudly for several seconds, gesturing wildly with her arms. Ma just sighs and says, "I already know all of that, but I sure do appreciate you stopping by."

The squirrel's shoulders droop with disappointment. She scampers back onto the fire escape, and Ma shuts the window to keep ash from blowing inside.

"You already know *what*, Ma? What's going on?" Mama asks, unable to hide her alarm.

Ma looks at me and holds up my half-eaten burger. "You gonna eat this?" When I shake my head, Ma takes a big bite, which prevents her from having to answer Mama's question.

"I'm surprised to see you, Ma," Trub says. "I thought the Supreme Council wanted all hands on deck in Chicago."

Ma takes another swig from her bottle of soda before responding. "Mrs. B. and Frank can handle Chicago." She thumps her chest a few times and burps before continuing. "We got a more serious situation that requires my attention." Ma flicks her eyes at me and adds, "A crisis, really."

I feel like Ma is pointing a finger straight at me. My cheeks start to burn. Have I done something wrong?

"We only did what the spiders told us to do!" I blurt out. "The phoenix and I destroyed the enchanted bridge."

Ma sighs heavily. "I know. But Ranadahy made that bridge out of ancient magic—power so pure it couldn't help but call to the Scourge." Ma rubs her eyes. I have never seen her so weary. "The collapse of the enchanted bridge required a massive surge of energy, which your feathery friend provided. But that bright burst led the Scourge straight to our world. It's here. And it will feed on every source of magic it can find."

Suddenly, my mouth is painfully dry. I take a sip of root beer and tell Ma, "I saw it before the phoenix pulled me through the gate. Sis was there, too. She dove right into the white mist. Sis can stop it from spreading, right?" When Ma doesn't respond, I turn to Trub. "There must be something we can do! The coven—Quayesha and Dutch. Are they still in Chicago? Maybe we should all go back to Palmara—right now!"

Mama glares at me. "Uh-uh. No way, Jax! Did you hear a word I just said?"

"These are my friends, Mama!" I plead. "I can't stay here and do nothing when they need my help." I'm not sure what I can actually do without the phoenix, but I have to at least try.

Ma places a heavy hand on my shoulder to calm me,

but her words have the opposite effect. "The Scourge has taken Sis hostage. It claims it's willing to negotiate, but I'm afraid only one thing can stop the Scourge."

"What's that?" I ask with a knot of hope and dread tightening in my chest.

"All who truly wish to keep magic alive must unite and defend our world against the Scourge. Your friend Ol-Korrok made this mess, but he had help." Ma looks at me, hard. "It's time for you to choose a side, Jax, because the witches are heading to war."

14

I am just as ancient as the phoenix, the spiders, the cobra, and the others that have been in this world almost from the very beginning. I have no satin feathers, no emerald eyes, no silken storyteller's tongue. But I am still part of this world.

The enchanted bridge summoned me and brought an end to my aimless wandering. The bridge brought me home.

I know they will not welcome me. I know my return has been dreaded for millennia. But this time, it will be different. I will take only what is offered to me. The hunger they fear will not overwhelm me. I will contain it. I will prove that I, too, can belong. I will not upset the balance. I will find my place in their world. Because their world is also mine. . . .

ACKNOWLEDGMENTS

Dragons in a Bag was inspired by my friend Marie's gift of several tiny dragons that I decided to carry in a mint tin inside my bag. But the series has continued because thousands of readers all over the world became ardent fans of Jaxon and his friends and committed to completing his journey. I am incredibly thankful for this support and appreciate how stories have kept us connected throughout the pandemic.

I used to insist that everything I wrote could be traced to something I saw on PBS. When COVID-19 made travel impractical, I gave up on a trip to Madagascar and instead relied on an amazing documentary that first aired on PBS in September 2020: *Islands of Wonder*. This episode helped me write *The Enchanted Bridge* in a way that honored the incredible geography and history of the oldest island in the world.

I didn't have inclusive fantasy fiction to read when I

was growing up, but I'm thankful that my father, George Hood, introduced me to tales of Anansi the trickster when I was a child. Much of my writing is an attempt to counter the stories from my youth that erased, diminished, or distorted all things African. As I explored African mythology, I looked to other Black authors for guidance. I thank Rena Barron and B. Sharise Moore for blazing a trail that I could follow across this new (to me) terrain. I hope this series and my use of "Afro-urban magic" can contribute to a fuller, more respectful understanding of the diverse cultures that originated on the continent and have been partially preserved by Black people throughout the Americas.

Shortly after *The Witch's Apprentice* was published, I learned that my editor was leaving Random House. Diane Landolf is an outstanding editor, and I am very grateful for the expertise and enthusiasm she brought to this series. Diane left me in very capable hands, and I'm glad that Tricia Lin joined me on the last leg of this journey. Kate Foster is my most trusted reader, and I thank her for all she has done to strengthen this series.

As I write this, at the start of 2022, Madagascar is facing near-famine conditions due to extreme drought in the southern part of the island. Rural Kenyans are confronting similar challenges as a direct result of global warming. Many countries in the developing world are being disproportionately impacted by fossil fuels burned for decades by wealthy industrialized nations like the United States. One of the most gratifying parts of my online interaction with educators has been to learn about innovative service projects inspired by the Dragons in a Bag series. I hope that as Jaxon's adventure draws to a close, students will continue to find ways to promote justice in their communities, in our country, and throughout our world.